THE ITALIAN, HIS PUP AND ME

—

ALISON ROBERTS

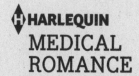

HARLEQUIN
MEDICAL
ROMANCE

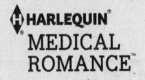

HARLEQUIN®
MEDICAL
ROMANCE™

Recycling programs
for this product may
not exist in your area.

ISBN-13: 978-1-335-59499-0

The Italian, His Pup and Me

Copyright © 2023 by Alison Roberts

Harlequin Enterprises ULC
22 Adelaide St. West, 41st Floor
Toronto, Ontario M5H 4E3, Canada
www.Harlequin.com

Printed in U.S.A.

Paramedics and Pups

Meet the first responders of Southern Sydney!

Best friends Jennifer Roden and Francesca Moretti
have dedicated themselves to helping others.
Long hours working as paramedics haven't left
much time for romance—which suits these friends
just fine! Jenny and Frankie each have their own
reasons to guard their hearts. But two gorgeous
new colleagues and a pair of rescue dogs are about
to turn their lives upside down! They might be
used to high-pressure rescues, but this time,
it's *their* hearts on the line...

Discover how Jenny finds her forever home with
small-town doc, and single dad, Dr. Rob Pierson in

Her Off-Limits Single Dad by Marion Lennox

And dive into the roller coaster of Frankie and
Nico's relationship in

The Italian, His Pup and Me by Alison Roberts

Both available now!

Dear Reader,

When I'm asked to write to you like this for the front of a new book, I think about the story and try to find something interesting to tell you. Usually, it's a personal link to the characters or setting or events in the story that will give me something to write about.

Not this time, though. It's not that I don't love Nico and Frankie. They're gorgeous and talented and they work in a profession I'm passionate about, being paramedics on an air-rescue base. The extra character of Bruce the dog was a real bonus because I'm such a dog lover, and Frankie and Nico are also both Italian and I got to spend a few happy hours of research reading recipes of one of my favorite cuisines.

But there's something else about this particular book that's special and that's because it's part of a duet with a very dear friend of mine, Marion Lennox. Writing can be a solitary, and sometimes lonely, career, so the friendships we make with fellow writers who share the same world are precious. Being able to work together and weave stories that can stand alone but also complement the other is a treat.

We started with two dogs that needed rescuing and it grew from there...

Happy reading—x2!

With love,

Alison xxx

Alison Roberts has been lucky enough to live in the South of France for several years recently but is now back in her home country of New Zealand. She is also lucky enough to write for the Harlequin Medical Romance line. A primary school teacher in a former life, she later became a qualified paramedic. She loves to travel and dance, drink champagne, and spend time with her daughter and her friends. Alison Roberts is the author of over one hundred books!

Books by Alison Roberts

Harlequin Medical Romance

Morgan Family Medics

Secret Son to Change His Life
How to Rescue the Heart Doctor

Two Tails Animal Refuge

The Vet's Unexpected Family

Miracle Baby, Miracle Family
A Paramedic to Change Her Life
One Weekend in Prague
The Doctor's Christmas Homecoming
Fling with the Doc Next Door

Visit the Author Profile page
at Harlequin.com for more titles.

For Linda
With very much love

**Praise for
Alison Roberts**

"Ms. Roberts has delivered a delightful read in this book where the chemistry between this couple was strong from the moment they meet…[and] the romance was heart-warming."

—*Harlequin Junkie* on
Melting the Trauma Doc's Heart

CHAPTER ONE

RULES *COULD* BE BROKEN, couldn't they?

When they were rules that you'd given yourself? And when there might be a very good reason to break them?

Like…if it seemed as if the perfect man had just walked into your life but you were not allowed to be remotely interested in him just because…

…because he was Italian?

Francesca Moretti let her breath out in a sigh that was melodramatic enough to attract the attention of the men sharing this table with her. She could feel several sets of eyes shifting to focus on her.

'What's up, Frankie?' Colin, shift manager for the South Sydney Air Rescue base, sounded genuinely concerned. 'Sounds like you just found out the world was ending. Did I miss a headline on that front page of the paper?'

'We've been on shift for too long with no action, that's all.' Mozzie, one of the Red Watch helicopter pilots shook his head. 'Interhospital transfers don't quite cut the mustard when our Frankie has such a low boredom threshold.'

'Not true.' Frankie waved a dismissive hand. 'I have no objection to transfers, even when they have an escort and we're just providing a taxi service. In theory, that is. And only in moderation, of course.' She put her empty coffee mug on top of the plate that had crumbs and melted cheese left over from her lunch toastie. 'But you're right. I've been sitting on my bum for too long and I just ate the biggest toasted cheese sandwich in the world. I'm going to go and lift some weights in the gym or something. It was windy enough this morning to bring tree branches down and it made it a bit dangerous to do my usual run through the bush reserve.'

'At least it's settled down now,' Mozzie said. 'Might still be a bit lumpy up there for a while, though.'

'Bring it on.' Frankie grinned. 'Lumpier the better as far as I'm concerned.'

She couldn't help shifting her gaze as she got to her feet.

To Mr Perfect.

The new addition to Red Watch—the helicopter rescue crew she had become a part of a couple of years ago now. Thanks to a relationship that had gone bad in a rather spectacular fashion, her best friend and colleague, Jenny, had thrown in the most exciting job in the world to go and be a paramedic in a small town much further south of Sydney and her position on the crew had been filled by…

Nico.

Nico Romano.

It wasn't just his name that was so obviously Italian. He had olive skin and wildly curly black hair that was long enough to need restraining in a kind of messy man bun thing at the back of his head while he was on duty. He had facial hair that was so neatly trimmed, in contrast, that it looked like designer stubble and his eyes were as dark as sin.

As dark as Frankie's were. And they were looking straight back at her. Frankie had to ignore the weird tingle that eye contact with this man had given her ever since they'd been introduced for the first time the other day. Now that they were working on their first shift together, she really needed to get it under firm control. She didn't actually know this man at all so this was vaguely reminiscent of a teenage crush on a movie star. Good grief…if she kept this up, she'd be putting a poster of the man on her bedroom wall and that thought was so ridiculous she could give herself the mental shove she needed to douse that tingle.

'You don't get air sick, do you, Nico?' She kept her tone light. Casual. Totally impersonal, even. 'Mozzie's quite happy to take on some pretty gnarly weather sometimes.'

'I never get sick,' he said. 'For any reason. I am…' He frowned. 'What's the expression? As healthy as a…hose?'

'That's a horse, mate.' Colin was laughing.

'That's what I said.'

'No…you said *hose*, which is what you water the garden with.'

'I thought he said *house*,' Mozzie said.

Everybody was laughing now. Except Frankie. Because Nico had an accent that was as Italian as everything else about him. He'd become a paramedic and gone on to work on helicopters in Milan and had only come to Australia to take up a position with an air ambulance in Queensland a handful of years ago but his English was as impressive as the CV that had put him at the top of a long list of contenders for the position of being part of this prestigious air rescue base.

Frankie had been born in Australia but she had grown up in an Italian community and been raised by her mother and grandmother. Both strong, independent women but they still bought into notions that should have been left behind in the old country generations ago. Frankie could actually hear an echo of her *nonna*'s voice in the back of her head.

'Why is it you want to keep doing a dangerous job like being a paramedic? In a helicopter, per amor del cielo! Find a nice Italian boy, Francesca, and settle down to have molte bambini. Give me some pronipoti before I die...'

Nico shrugged off the laughter with a resigned shrug and went back to reading the SOPs—Standard Operating Procedures—for his new base. Frankie knew he'd done an initiation protocol during her last few days off and he'd been working already with an Australian helicopter crew as a paramedic so he should fit in seamlessly with her crew, but the glue that held people together in stressful situations wasn't just about having expertise in invasive interventions in a trauma case, for example, or being skilled at winch operations.

Colin lifted his hand in a wave as he went back to his office. Mozzie said he was off to do another check on his beloved helicopter—a brand new Airbus H145 that was his pride and joy. Ricky—an aircrew officer, whose role included assisting the pilot, paramedics or doctors with medical care, looking after equipment and operating the winch—reached for Frankie's empty coffee mug and plate to take to the dishwasher with his lunch dishes.

'You don't have to tidy up after me, Ricky.'

'And there I was thinking that was the only reason you kept me around, Frankie.'

Frankie rolled her eyes but she was smiling. Red Watch was a tight team and the reason for that was the X factor in whether a crew became tight enough for trust to be automatic. The cohesion of any group like this depended on the personalities of the people as much as, or possibly even more than any other factor.

The jury was still out on Nico Romano. Except that Frankie knew she shouldn't even be *on* the jury because she was clinging to some rebellious streak that she'd developed decades ago, thanks to her *nonna* and the community she'd grown up within. A stupid rule she'd made into a sacred vow and stuck to ever since. She also knew that it wasn't remotely acceptable to be judging someone simply on their appearance, nationality or accent. She had to give the man a chance, for heaven's sake. She didn't actually know anything about him.

Except that he was drop-dead gorgeous.

And he could do strange things to her body just by *looking* at her...

Oh, help...

Frankie had never been more grateful for the vibration and beep of the pager attached to her belt. She could see Colin coming out of the office at the same time and he had a look on his face that she could read instantly.

There was an emergency somewhere within their reach and they were about to get dispatched to where they were needed most. Frankie had no idea where it might be or how serious it was but she could feel her adrenaline levels rising fast. This was what she loved about this job. You started every single mission not knowing what kind of challenges you could be up against, but that only made it more exciting. The goal was always the same. To help people in what might be the biggest challenge they would ever face.

To stay alive.

* * *

Nico Romano was in one of his favourite places.

Sitting in the open doorway of a helicopter, with one foot balanced on the skid, trusting the strap he had hooked to the roof of the cabin as he leaned out, trying to be the first to spot their target amongst the challenging landscape below.

Finally, after a couple of trauma cases that were satisfying but pretty routine, they were way out in the Central Blue Mountains, west of Sydney, on a mission that was promising to be a lot less ordinary. They had landed some distance away from the scene location to rendezvous with the Blue Mountains Police, configure the helicopter for a winch operation and get all the details they could on the incident they'd been dispatched to. It was a mission that was already ticking a lot of boxes near the top of a job satisfaction scoresheet for Nico.

The incident had happened halfway down a canyon, which added all sorts of challenges to extract the patient. The injured hiker's accident might have only resulted in a probable ankle fracture but the sixty-five-year-old man had since developed chest pain and other symptoms that suggested he might be having a heart attack, so it could prove to be a challenge medically as well as logistically. They had hovered over the scene before landing, long enough to make a plan of action, and Mozzie reckoned he could perch a skid on the edge of a ledge, which would let the medic jump out and save the time it would take to winch them down and then back up with the patient attached to him.

Best of all, it was Nico who was going to be the one leaping out onto that ledge.

It had been Frankie's suggestion how they would decide who would take the lead in what was likely to be the last mission and the first winch operation for this shift. She'd caught Nico's glance as they moved swiftly back to the helicopter.

'Want to do the winch?'

'If you're happy, yes, absolutely.' He gave her a quick smile. 'But I wouldn't want you to get bored on your first day working with me.'

She didn't exactly smile back but there was a gleam in her eyes that looked like approval and that was a win all by itself, given the cool reception he'd noted in his new colleague up till now.

'Rock, paper, scissors, then?'

Nobody could hear them over the crescendo of the helicopter rotors gaining speed.

It took no more than five seconds. Nobody would have noticed the swift hand gestures either. And Nico had won, scissors over paper, no doubt thanks to the many games of *sasso, carta, forbici* he had played with his sisters to also settle arguments about who got to have the best treat being offered or first turn at an activity they all wanted to do.

Frankie reminded him very much of his sisters, to be honest, with that long, curly black hair that was barely tamed by a braid and dark eyes beneath a heavy fringe and a luxuriant tangle of eyelashes. She might sound like an Australian but there was no mistaking her Italian genes. She was confident. A bit loud. She used her hands a lot when she was talking and…she talked—and laughed—a lot.

Nico didn't want to like that. He most certainly didn't want to find it as attractive as he seemed to be finding it. Attraction like this was dangerous and Nico knew exactly why he had alarm bells already sounding, and why he needed to shut it down before it could even start. That way, it could never escalate into something too big to resist. You wouldn't start trusting someone enough to fall in love with them and you could avoid ending up with that trust shattered, along with any shred of self-esteem.

Nico had made that mistake once before, when he'd fallen for Sofia—his first love— hard enough to marry her and it had, quite literally, scarred him for life. Emotionally *and* physically.

Never again.

It was all in the past now. That longing to find his soul mate. To be the best husband ever and to have his own children growing up as part of the beloved new generation of the Romano family. That dream, like the kind of trust he had put in the person he had chosen to share that future, no longer existed.

The yearning could still come out of hiding occasionally, however, no matter how unwelcome it was, but Nico had learned how to deflect it, if he couldn't dismiss it entirely at times. He could find a reason for its appearance that was not going to mess with how happy he was with his new life.

He missed his sisters, that was all—along with the rest of his family. Maybe this attraction wasn't sexual at all—it could be simply a comforting familiarity to have someone who shared his cultural heritage as a member of his new crew. It didn't go both ways, that was for sure. There was also no mistaking the suspicion with which Frankie had been regarding him since they were introduced a few days ago. Had she sensed that he was drawn to her and was making it very clear that she wasn't interested? It obviously wasn't going to be an instant friendship after bonding over pizza or something, but Nico was hoping that his performance on this next job might at least make him more welcome on her crew.

And that was all he wanted from Frankie Moretti—a professional relationship—no matter how attractive she might be or how easily she might be able to cure any vestige of homesickness after his years away from Italy. Even friendship could well get too close to a boundary Nico had no intention of crossing. With any woman, but especially not with someone like Frankie.

Oddio… She would be the last woman on earth who could change his mind about that, because it wasn't just his sisters that she reminded him of, was it?

It was every Italian woman.

Including Sofia.

Especially Sofia, thanks to the level of attraction that had been almost a kick in his gut when they'd been introduced.

But it was okay. It might be a bigger challenge than he was used to handling but he knew he wasn't in any danger. History was not going to be allowed to repeat itself.

Mozzie's control of the aircraft was impressive as they approached the incident scene again. So was the landscape below, with a waterfall between two rocky cliffs which were far enough apart to let the helicopter drop between them and had the advantage of protecting them from any wind gusts higher up. With one skid delicately touching the very edge of a large outcrop of rocks, Nico was able to jump out, with a backpack containing medical supplies and a winch harness for a patient. An upward glance as Mozzie took the helicopter up to hover nearby, well above the cliffs, showed Frankie leaning out to watch Nico.

His patient wasn't far away, on the ground, leaning against another member of his hiking group who had climbed down to care for him until help arrived.

'I'm Nico. I hear you've got a sore ankle and some chest pain?' Nico could already see the deformity of the man's ankle that indicated a dislocation and probable fracture as well.

'I didn't take his boot off,' the man's companion said. 'I didn't want to hurt Martin here, and I thought it might be providing a bit of a splint.'

'Good thinking.' Nico nodded. 'I'll give him some pain relief before we do anything to his foot.' There was something else that was more of a concern right now. 'Tell me about this chest pain, Martin,' he said. 'Have you ever had anything like this before?'

'No. It's right here.' He put a hand on the centre of his chest. 'And it goes into my neck and up into my jaw as well.'

'If I give you a scale of zero to ten, with zero being no pain and ten being the worst you can think of, what number would you give this pain?'

'Ten. It's worse than my ankle.'

Nico nodded. 'I'm going to put a needle in your hand and give you something for the pain and then we're going to get you up into our helicopter as quickly as possible, okay?'

'Okay...'

Martin lay back against his friend. He looked grey, Nico noted, and he was sweating profusely. He couldn't do an ECG until he got his patient on board but the urgency to do so was high. Nico opened his kit and pulled items out rapidly.

'Are you allergic to any drugs that you know of, Martin?'

'No.'

'Do you have any medical conditions I should know about? High blood pressure, asthma, diabetes…?'

'No.'

'Okay…sharp scratch…there we go.' Nico secured the line and drew up the drugs he needed to administer. With effective pain relief on board, he removed the heavy boot and splinted the foot and ankle and, with the help of Martin's friend, he got his patient into a harness. They were able to get him standing on one leg, with the support of being clipped to Nico's harness.

'You need to get right back.' Nico had to raise his voice to a shout over the sound of the helicopter's rotors after he radioed that he was ready for pickup, and the friend began scrambling back up the cliff to where other hiking club members were huddled. The sound was deafening as Mozzie hovered between the cliffs again and a winch line was being lowered. Ricky was operating the winch and Frankie was where he'd been earlier, with one foot on the skid, waiting to help get their patient on board.

It took very little time. As soon as they

were on board the door was closed and Mozzie gained altitude and turned back towards the city.

Nico and Frankie both began to work on Martin, attaching chest pads and other monitoring equipment.

'Symptoms strongly suggestive of ischaemic chest pain,' Nico said. 'No history of cardiac problems. We're not going to get an accurate twelve-lead ECG en route but I can see significant ST elevation on the single lead rhythm strip.'

'Oxygen saturation's below ninety-four percent,' Frankie said. 'I'll put some oxygen on.'

'Blood pressure?'

'One seventy over ninety. Heart rate's sixty-two. Is he on any medication?'

'No.'

'What's our flight time to the nearest PCI unit?'

'That'll be St Mary's. At least twenty-five minutes, I'd guess. Mozzie?'

But Mozzie was busy with a call from the South Coast Emergency Response Centre that controlled the dispatch of all emergency service vehicles and aircraft. Nico could hear him telling the control room that they were unavailable for at least the next thirty minutes and that he'd update them as soon as they were free.

'How's that pain in your chest now, Martin?'

'Not so bad...'

'Can you score it for me? Out of ten like we did before?'

'About a six?'

'I can give you some more medication for that.'

'I feel a bit sick.'

'I'll give you something for that as well. Sorry, it's a bit bumpy up here today.'

Nico had to focus to be able to draw up the drugs and administer them with the sideways slipping of the helicopter in conditions that were a little turbulent again and then he had to pause to attach the syringe to the plug before injecting the drugs when they hit a sudden drop. He glanced up at Frankie.

'Lumpy enough for you?'

'I'm not complaining.' Frankie was watching his movements and her half smile suggested she was also not complaining about his handling of the conditions and their patient.

They both shifted their gaze to the monitor as an alarm sounded. Martin's heartrate had dropped below sixty into a bradycardia.

'Level of consciousness is dropping,' Frankie warned. 'Martin?' She shook their patient's shoulder. 'Can you hear me?'

But Martin's eyes were closed and his head slumped to one side. And Nico could see the ominous wide, bizarre complexes on the ECG trace that suddenly deteriorated into a pattern that was no more than an uncoordinated squiggle.

'He's in VF,' he said tersely. 'Stand clear, Frankie. I'm going to defibrillate him.'

'Want me to land?' Mozzie could hear what was being said between the crew members. He knew how urgent this was and Nico could feel the helicopter losing altitude already.

'No. We would lose too much time. I'm happy to do it now. Charging to maximum joules.'

Nico caught the startled glances from both Frankie and Ricky and he understood that they might be concerned. Defibrillating during flight was riskier than on land, especially in turbulent conditions, but he had done this before and he was confident. Trying to do effective CPR in a vibrating aircraft for as long as it took to find a suitable landing site and put the chopper down would eat too much into the time it was possible to keep heart muscle alive.

'Stay clear,' he warned the others again. 'Hang onto something in case we hit a bump.'

He pressed the shock button and Martin's body jerked but the interference on the monitor screen settled to reveal he was still in the fatal cardiac rhythm of ventricular fibrillation.

'Start CPR, please, Frankie. I will place an LMA. If that's not adequate, I'll intubate.' Nico reached for the laryngeal airway that would be much easier to place than intubating in these cramped conditions. He had to ride the movement of a downdraught before he could insert the airway and fill the cushion with air with the attached syringe to secure it. He clipped a bag mask onto the airway with a practised swiftness and a quick squeeze showed the chest rising adequately. Thankfully, they already had IV access so Nico could draw up the drugs needed and administer them before they had another attempt to defibrillate their patient. Moments later, Nico braced himself to snap open an ampoule of adrenaline and slide a needle in to draw up the drug without stabbing himself in the process. He could see that Frankie was also bracing herself and that she was doing an impressive job of keeping her chest compressions fast and deep enough to be effective. Ricky had managed to fit into a space where he could be providing ventilations and vital oxygen.

Somewhere, in the very back of Nico's brain, was a passing reminder that he'd hoped this mission would make him a welcome addition to this crew.

He hadn't expected it to be quite this dramatic. And now he had to focus completely and do his utmost to keep their patient alive.

Wow...

Just...wow...

Frankie slid yet another glance at their new crew member as they flew back to base. They were already late to finish their shift but what a way to complete a first day. Nico had shown himself to be not only confident but even more capable than any one of them might have hoped he would be. He had undoubtedly saved a man's life today. The second in-flight defibrillation on Martin had restored a perfusing rhythm and he was actually waking up as they landed on the roof of St Mary's Hospital in the western suburbs of Sydney, where he would be fast-tracked to the catheter laboratory to have his coronary arteries unblocked and prevent any further damage to his heart.

'I've never done that,' Frankie confessed. 'Defibrillated in-flight, that is. Or intubated, for that matter. I've always done it prior to transfer. Or we've touched down somewhere.'

The corners of Nico's mouth lifted a little. 'It's no different to doing it on the ground,' he said. 'You just need to be a little more careful, that's all. Especially when it's lumpy.'

'It saved so much time. It could have tipped the balance to getting him back. Not only getting his heart going again, but fast enough to prevent any hypoxic brain injury.'

'I couldn't believe it when he opened his eyes and tried to pull out the LMA.' Ricky was grinning. 'Good job, Nico.'

Nico just shrugged. 'It was a team effort.' He turned to look out of his window as Mozzie brought the helicopter down on the big cross painted outside the South Sydney Air Rescue hangar.

Frankie let her gaze rest on him a little longer this time. So Nico Romano wasn't just gorgeous to look at. He was courageous and competent and remarkably modest about his talents, and her being attracted to him had just tipped into something a little more significant.

Good grief…was she in danger of falling in love with this man already?

It was just as well they were colleagues on the same crew because that was as good as an ironclad backup rule. Getting involved with an Italian man might be the first on the list of Frankie's no-go areas, but someone she had to work with this closely was definitely a close second. She had seen all too often the damage that could be wrought in a career by an ill-advised romantic liaison and she was not about to risk any aspect of the job she loved so much. She only had to remember the reason her friend Jenny had felt forced to leave this air rescue base and that disastrous fallout from a relationship gone very wrong hadn't even been with someone she worked with every day.

She wanted to echo Ricky's praise and tell Nico that he'd done well today but, for some reason, Frankie felt very uncharacteristically shy. Maybe because she knew she'd been a little less than entirely welcoming and was now somewhat embarrassed about it? Deliberately putting up a barrier hadn't been only because Nico was Italian and far too good-looking. Frankie had already been missing working with her best friend.

'… Jenny?'

'What?' Frankie's glance swerved towards Mozzie, who was catching up behind her. She had clearly missed something he'd been saying.

'Isn't Willhua where Jenny moved to?'

'Yes...' Frankie's eyebrows shot up. Had Mozzie been reading her mind? 'Why?'

'I was just talking to Donna in Control and they're about to drop a new job on us.'

'But we're way over time to finish our shift already. It's dark...'

'There's no one else available. We got a call about this one when you lot were in the middle of saving that guy from his cardiac arrest. A truck went over a cliff just out of Willhua. The response crew got a status one patient out from the wreck and took him to the local hospital, but apparently they think there may be another person involved. Some guy called Bruce. They just want us to go and have a look. We might be able to see something from out to sea that they can't see from where they are on the road and, if there is someone down there, they'd rather not leave them until daylight when they can get climbers down.'

'Okay...' Frankie nodded. She lifted her helmet to put it back on but Mozzie shook his head.

'We might be going for just a look-see, but if we do spot something we need to be prepared. Could be a body retrieval and it might end up being a winch operation. It could be wet. We'll keep the crew minimal so Ricky can go home but at least one of you'd better get a suit on.'

Frankie caught Nico's glance. He was grinning and she saw his hand form a fist by his side. She followed his example. Mozzie was looking straight ahead and couldn't see what they were doing. Holding Nico's gaze, she pumped her fist, once, twice… On the third time she kept it as a fist. Nico had made a V sign with his fingers for scissors. It had taken only a couple of seconds this time and Frankie's rock had won. Nico conceded defeat with a single nod but held Frankie's gaze for a moment longer and, in that flick of time, she could feel…something that had nothing to do with that tingle.

The first strand of the kind of bond you wanted to have with a colleague?

The first beat of a friendship?

Whatever…

It felt good.

'Five minutes,' she called over her shoulder as her pager sounded and she broke into a run. 'Don't go anywhere without me.'

CHAPTER TWO

THE FARM TRUCK had apparently been initially caught halfway down the cliff but had since moved because it had only been a tree that was keeping it relatively stable. The tide was in and waves would be breaking over the rocks on the shoreline and probably splashing high enough to make it cold and wet if a medic needed to be winched down to a victim. It was quite possible they might end up retrieving a body from the ocean, as Mozzie had suggested, in which case the medic would actually have to be in the water.

Which was why Frankie had put on her wet suit before they even took off from the base. The section of the road where the accident had happened was already closed so the helicopter would be able to land on the road, if necessary, to prepare for a winch operation by removing any unessential equipment, like the stretcher and equipment packs, but

Frankie didn't want to be trying to squeeze into a wet suit at that point.

In front of Nico…

She closed the zips on the ankles of her suit and put her wet shoes on, with their extra ankle support and the neoprene insoles to absorb the impact of climbing over rocks. She was putting on her helmet as she walked out to the landing pad, where the helicopter rotors were already gaining speed and its identification lights flashing. Mozzie had his night vision goggles in place over his helmet and Nico handed Frankie a pair as she climbed on board and slid the door shut behind her. Moments later they were lifting clear of the ground.

'Flight time?'

'Less than thirty minutes,' Mozzie responded.

'Any more info?'

'Not yet. Local cop is trying to have a good look before we get there but it sounds like he's only got a torch so I wouldn't think he'll be able to see much.'

'It's very close to Willhua Rocks, right?' Frankie was tapping the screen of her tablet to bring up all the information they had so far. 'That's where Jenny's taken that paramedic position. I know she wasn't due to start her new job for a day or two, but she might have been involved with the response effort already.'

'Jenny?' Nico raised his eyebrows.

'The medic you've replaced on the crew.'

'Why did she leave?' Nico was looking down at his own tablet. 'Looks like this Willhua's barely a dot on the map. A village. Bit of a contrast to working with air rescue, isn't it?'

'A bit of quiet time is probably just what she needs,' Frankie said. Not that she was going to divulge information her best friend wouldn't want her to share, but Nico would no doubt hear about the scandal of Jenny's relationship with the married CEO of South Sydney Air Rescue anyway. 'She had some personal stuff she needed to get away from.'

Nico's smile was wry. 'I understand. Personally, I find that keeping too busy to have time to think works better than going to quiet places.'

Frankie blinked at the idea that Mr Perfect might have found it necessary to keep super busy in order to get through the heartbreak of a crashed relationship. It was more believable that he had needed to fight off the hordes of women who would be desperate to attract his attention. Like she could be if she let herself step into that space?

She shook that disturbing thought off by turning to look down as they left the brightly lit edges of south Sydney behind them to head down the coast. The night vision goggles made the world look green and black and any lights shone like small stars. The lights from houses got further and further apart and cars moving on the coastal road made it easy to see where the land ended and the sea began.

They didn't need to wear the night vision goggles when they reached the GPS coordinates of the accident scene. Mozzie activated the 'night sun'—a searchlight attached to the front lefthand side of the helicopter that had the power of thirty to forty million candles. They hovered just above the waves at the point before they started to break, taking in the scene from the sea side. Frankie clipped a safety line to an anchor and opened the side door so she could sit on the edge above the skid and peer right beneath the helicopter. Nico had also clipped himself onto a safety line and was standing behind her, leaning over her shoulder.

The wrecked truck wasn't halfway down the cliff now. It had slipped further and was lying on its back like a dead turtle amongst huge rocks that might be well clear of the waves in low tide but had white spray cutting visibility now and water reaching the level of the wheels every time a wave washed in.

'If anyone was still in the vehicle, they would have drowned long ago,' Frankie said.

'The vehicle was cleared before the local emergency services left the scene.'

'Doesn't necessarily mean that somebody didn't try and get back to it later. What if they had a head injury and it seemed like a safe place to head for?'

'Fair call.' Nico nodded. 'Can we get the light higher, please, Mozzie, to where the truck was to start with?'

'No worries.'

The centre of the intense beam of light from the night sun moved up the cliff as the helicopter gained height.

'That must be the tree that the truck was caught on.' Frankie could see the pale scars of gouged bark and a freshly broken branch. She turned her head, trying to imagine where a body might end up if it had been thrown from this vehicle on its way over the edge of the cliff or bouncing against the rocks and sparse vegetation on its slide towards that tree.

And then she caught her breath.

'I can see something. And I think I can see it moving...'

'Where?' Nico was leaning further out of the helicopter. Frankie could actually feel the warmth of his breath on the side of her neck. Or maybe it was just his body heat?

'Behind that group of rocks at about seven o'clock. Maybe two metres down from the tree. There's a bit of scrub and there's something white...'

'Can't see a thing.'

'There...' Frankie pointed. 'It looks like... I'm not sure. A tee shirt sleeve, maybe? A bit of white clothing, anyway. I think someone's waving at us. Calling for help...' She was wriggling back into the cabin. 'Mozzie? Is the road okay to touch down so we can configure for a winch job?'

Mozzie took the helicopter higher and they all scanned the area for potential hazards like power lines or loose debris. A police car with its lights flashing was further up the road near a bend, to prevent any approaching traffic getting onto this section of the road. What looked like a tow truck was doing the same thing in the opposite direction and there was another police car beside it that was most likely the transport for members of the Serious Crash Squad who would be investigating this accident.

Mozzie put the helicopter down gently on the empty tarmac between those vehicles and they quickly set up to winch.

'You happy with operating the winch, Nico?'

'Of course. Why would I not be?' Nico's tone was slightly defensive and he was frowning.

'Just checking.' Frankie clipped a carabiner to her harness and met his gaze straight-on. It was her life that would be—literally—on the line if something went wrong. 'This is a new setup for you.'

'It's exactly the setup I was working with in my last position. I double-checked everything on my initiation.'

Frankie would have understood if Nico was offended by the unspoken concern she might have about his skills, given they had no backup by the presence of a crewman, but the way his expression softened told her that he understood exactly how much trust she was putting in someone she hadn't worked with for more than a matter of hours.

'I'll keep you safe, Frankie,' he said. 'I promise.'

Mozzie was just as responsible for keeping her safe and he had earned Frankie's complete trust long ago. Within a short time Frankie found herself being slowly lowered on the end of a wire towards the ledge with the scarred tree and its broken branches. She was carrying only a harness that could be used to extract either a living patient or a body, but nothing else. If any treatment was needed, down this cliff in the darkness wasn't the time or place to be doing it. Mozzie could lift her straight up to the road above and put her down before landing again himself.

Frankie watched the approaching rocks of the cliffside.

'Ten metres,' she told the crew through the microphone in her helmet. 'Six…four… two… Okay…' Frankie could feel her feet were secure on the rocks. 'I'm down. Unhooking now…'

She needed to be free of the winch line quickly so there was no danger of it getting tangled with the remains of the nearby tree and she held the winch hook high and away from her body before using a signal with her other hand to let Nico know he could wind it back in. Mozzie moved the helicopter further away so that she wasn't being buffeted by the downdraught from the rotors, and that was when Frankie took a deep breath and began to scan the area.

She was alone on a steep cliff. In the dark. She could see the inky darkness of unforgiving rocks below her and the foam of crashing waves, sparkling in the light the helicopter was still providing. It should have been terrifying but Frankie knew the best way to push any fear back. She just had to focus on why she was here. She'd seen movement. Something white. Something that might be a person in very real trouble.

Except…it wasn't.

Frankie carefully climbed down past the scrub that had managed to grow amongst the rocks, thickly enough to provide both a cushion effect to break a fall and a cover to make it hard to be seen. The patch of white she'd seen from above was not a piece of clothing, however. It was the tip of a long and very fluffy tail that belonged to quite a big black and white dog. A dog who was looking straight at her as she parted the branches of the scruffy bush.

'Oh…' Frankie had never faced quite this situation before. The dog looked frightened and was trying to move. Towards her or further away? Her first thought was that if it moved too far it could quickly be in danger of falling further down the cliff onto those rocks. She reached for the thick leather collar around its neck. She could see something written on the collar, probably in permanent marker ink. *BRUCE*...

'Oh...' she said again, more loudly this time.

'What is it?' Nico's voice in the headphones of her helmet sounded like he was standing right beside her.

'I've found him. Bruce.'

'Status?'

'Um...' Bruce the dog was still looking very scared. He was damp from windblown sea spray and was probably cold and when he tried to get up in response to her focused attention she heard him whine and saw that he couldn't put weight on a front leg, but he didn't seem to be badly injured otherwise. 'Category four, I guess. Three at the most. He might have a leg injury but it doesn't appear obviously fractured.'

'So he can climb out himself? And help get the harness on?'

'No, I'll need to put the harness on him.' Frankie was thinking fast. Risking your own safety for an animal was not an approved part of any SOPs but she couldn't leave this poor dog here all night, waiting for someone to try and climb down to rescue him in daylight. 'It's okay… I can manage.'

She stroked the dog's head. 'It's okay, Bruce,' she told him. 'I'm here to help. You're going to be okay…you just need to trust me.'

And Bruce, bless him, seemed to understand. Or maybe he was just too frightened to protest as she put the dog's legs through the holes in a harness designed for humans and then strapped it tightly enough to be secure before attaching it to her own harness and pulling herself, with the not inconsiderable extra weight, back to the clearer space further up. She signalled for the winch line to be lowered again and it was then that she heard the odd pause in communication and knew that Nico and probably Mozzie were both trying to work out what was going on.

'What is that?' Nico sounded bewildered. 'Is Bruce a *child*?'

'He's a dog.'

There was another silence. Frankie clipped the winch hook to her harness and signalled that she was ready to be lifted. 'Put us up on the road,' she said. 'We can sort it out there.'

The local police officer, two officers from the Serious Crash Squad and the tow truck driver seemed to find it a bit of a joke that a multi-million-dollar helicopter and its highly trained crew had used their impressive resources to rescue an extremely scruffy-looking farm dog. They weren't, however, about to offer to take it off their hands.

The police officer walked off, laughing. 'He might like a ride in the helicopter back to the city,' he suggested. 'I better go and sort that traffic that's piling up.'

There were only two cars behind where he'd blocked the road with his police car.

'We've got a job to do,' one of the crash investigators said and went in the same direction.

The tow truck driver just shook her head and walked in the opposite direction. 'I'm not allowed dogs in my truck,' she said. 'And there's no point in me hanging around. We're not about to pull that wreck up from the rocks in the dark.'

'Can you have a look at him?' Frankie asked Nico. 'And see if he's hurt?'

'I'm not a vet,' Nico protested. 'I don't know anything about treating dogs. Are you telling me you normally take animals as patients as well as people?'

'No, of course not.' Nico's reaction was disappointing. 'But I couldn't leave him down the cliff. And we can't just leave him on the road, can we?'

'We can't just use an air rescue helicopter to take him anywhere else. I'm sure there must be some regulations about that.'

Bruce was lying on the tarmac. A bit hunched. He looked as though he was avoiding any direct eye contact as both Nico and Mozzie looked down at him.

Mozzie shrugged. 'He looks a bit cold. I'll grab a towel so we can get him a bit drier. It won't hurt to take a look at him, will it?'

'I'll try and get hold of Jenny and find out if there's a local vet or rescue centre that could come and get him.'

'Good thinking.' Mozzie nodded. 'But make it quick, yeah? It'd be quite nice to get home some time soon and I need to let Control know what's happening.'

It took only a couple of taps on the screen of her phone to call Jenny, and Frankie found herself holding her breath, realising how much she was already missing working with someone who'd been a colleague until only a matter of days ago, but so much more than that as well. Her closest friend.

The note in Jenny's voice as she answered the call made it obvious she'd been on tenterhooks, waiting for news on the missing victim.

'What gives?' she asked.

'You're not going to believe this,' Frankie told her. 'Bruce is a dog.'

'A *dog*?' There was relief in her voice now.

'A great big hairy dog,' Frankie confirmed. 'I'm no expert but Mozzie's spent time on farms and he reckons he might be a bearded collie. He and Nico are trying to dry him off a bit.'

'I'm not really surprised,' Jenny said. 'We already rescued one dog that was with Charlie. Where was this one? Why didn't I see it?'

'He was curled up in a tight ball, hiding amongst rocks and scrub not far from that tree that the truck was initially caught on. He must have been thrown clear when it first went over the cliff. He's black and white— it was only because I caught a glimpse of the white hair that we found him. He would have been totally hidden from view when you pulled that guy out.' Frankie pulled in a breath. 'Speaking of whom… Condition?'

'He's just died.'

'Oh, no… I'm so sorry, love, and on your first day.'

'My first day's supposed to be on Monday.'

'And you wanted a quiet life.' Frankie's

heart went out to her friend. The silence on the other end of the line made her think that dwelling on the bad news would only make it worse.

'Our reports were that a fatality was likely.' Frankie knew Mozzie wanted to get back to base as soon as possible. She really couldn't spend too much more time on this phone call. 'Jen, we still have a problem. The Serious Crash Squad got mobilised when your local cop pinged this as a possible fatality. They're here now but they don't want anything to do with the dog. They suggested we drop him off to you so the local vet can check him out.'

'Is he injured?'

'Not sure.' Frankie turned her head to see Nico and Mozzie crouched beside the dog— dark shapes against the backlight of the police vehicle's headlights. 'Nico's having a look now but I'd be surprised if he wasn't hurt. Pretty rough ground for a fall.'

'Who's Nico?'

'Your replacement on Red Watch.'

'Is he nice?'

'He's Italian.'

'Oh…'

They both knew that was the end of a conversation they didn't have time for, anyway.

'Do you know if the local vet will be available?' Frankie asked.

'There's no vet in Willhua.'

'Can he go to Charlie's family?'

'I have no idea who they might be,' Jen said. 'Frankie, can you take him on to Sydney? I seem to be stuck with the other one—Stumpy—and I can't cope with two injured dogs.'

Frankie bit her lip. She knew how well that suggestion might go down, after Nico's reaction to rescuing a dog in the first place. She watched the men as they got to their feet to move back towards the helicopter. Nico picked up Bruce, who was now wrapped in a blanket, and he turned his head to signal to Frankie that it was time to go. He probably assumed that she had finished making the arrangement to drop the dog at Willhua hospital's landing pad.

Frankie could hear Jenny talking to someone else. Saying something about Bruce being another dog. That he was safe. She didn't want to tell her that it might not be easy to persuade her crew to take Bruce back to Sydney with them, even though there was no chance they would be dispatched to any other jobs tonight. Jenny had already had a rough day and Frankie wasn't about to make it any harder.

'Frankie, I need to go,' Jenny said. 'Stumpy's got lacerations and grazes, and Rob's going to help me sort her out.'

'Who's Rob?'

'Cut it out.' There was an understanding of why Frankie was asking. This just wasn't the time or place. 'But can you take Bruce?'

'I'll see what I can do.' Frankie didn't want to make any promises. 'There's already a discussion about having a dog in the chopper.'

'But that would be a yes? That's great.' Jen made it sound like a done deal. 'If and when we find relatives we can tell them he's in the best of hands and to contact you.'

'Jen...'

'I need to go.' Jen wasn't listening. 'Love you.'

'Love you too,' Frankie murmured. But the screen of her phone had already gone dark. Jenny had gone and it was time for Frankie to move as well. The rotors on the helicopter were starting to gain speed and she ducked her head until she climbed in and slid the door shut behind her.

Nico was strapped into his seat, with his arms still around the big dog who was draped over his knees. Bruce had his head leaning on Nico's chest as he gazed upwards and it looked for all the world as if they were having a private conversation.

'There's no vet in Willhua,' Frankie told him. 'They've asked if we'll take him back to Sydney.'

She'd expected a flat-out refusal. A lecture on what was and wasn't acceptable for the crew of an air rescue helicopter to be using their valuable resources for. Instead, all Frankie got was a solemn nod.

'No worries,' Nico said. 'I'll look after him.'

Maybe it was something in the way he was holding the dog. Or the way they'd been looking at each other. Or perhaps it was just something in the tone of his voice that had made his words sound like a vow. He had promised to keep Frankie safe on the winch. And he had done exactly that...

Whatever it was, it felt disconcertingly as if Frankie had just stepped a little bit closer to falling in love with Nico Romano. She clipped the buckles of her safety belts together and then she leaned back as they took off—trying to remind herself that, unlike rescuing a dog instead of a human, there were some rules that she could never afford to break.

But then Nico raised his head and she caught a glimpse of the look he'd probably been sharing with that dog. Dark, dark eyes that had a glimmer of a stereotype she'd been running away from for ever, where the man was the dominant partner in a relationship and his needs came first. There was another side to that coin, though, wasn't there? That ability to be so passionate. Devoted. A keeper of promises and the protector of the most important things in the world—the people that were loved. Family...

And in that heartbeat of time Frankie had the disturbing idea that maybe she'd been wrong all along. Ever since she'd made that stupid rule.

Worse, she now had a thirty-minute flight with no patient to care for, so there was no distraction from letting her mind drift into a bit of fantasy.

What if Nico fell in love with *her*?

What if he was as ready as she was to start a family? Frankie was only in her early thirties, but the ticking of her biological clock was noticeably louder these days and she was hearing it more and more often during any job that involved children and especially babies.

She wanted a big, classically Italian kind

of family like she'd never had. Frankie closed her eyes and could almost hear the noise and see the happy chaos of this fantasy family that was big enough that none of the children would ever feel lonely or left out.

Like she had…

CHAPTER THREE

'SO THIS IS GOOD. There's no sign of any broken bones. I think he's just badly bruised on this front leg and there could be some ligament damage in both joints. It's pretty swollen around the carpus, which is the equivalent to his wrist, and the elbow is sore as well. I'll put a bandage on the whole leg but he'll need to keep his weight off it as much as possible for at least a week.'

The vet's name was Phoebe. She had blue eyes and long blonde hair that was pulled back into a ponytail and she had seemed more than happy to welcome a patient at a quiet time on her night shift at the after-hours emergency clinic when Nico walked in—still in his uniform—with the large dog in his arms.

It was just the kind of scenario that Nico might have taken advantage of in the past few years—when he had finally sorted a totally new life with a career that he could focus on with a passion that made life away from work almost irrelevant. Or maybe it had just taken more time to be confident that he could *make* love and still keep himself completely safe from *falling* in love. A sex life was a physical need, after all, like eating. Fortunately, Nico had discovered that he could go for considerable periods of time without starving and any woman he'd got that close to in the last ten years or so hadn't been put off by knowing it was only ever a casual thing. An occasional treat—like a takeout meal instead of home cooking?

Phoebe looked like she wouldn't be put off either, even if it was just a one-off occasion, but Nico wasn't feeling any tingle of attraction at all, and it *wasn't* simply because she didn't have dark hair and dark eyes like Frankie. Not at all. It was because things were different right now. This was about Bruce.

'He seems well fed. I'd say he's about six to eight years old and he's definitely a farm dog.' Phoebe smiled at Nico. 'He kind of smells like a sheep, doesn't he?'

'So he's going to be okay?'

'Physically, yes. He's a bit traumatised, which is understandable after the accident, but it says a lot about his personality that he's not at all aggressive when he's this scared. I think he's a nice dog. If the owner's family doesn't claim him, I'm sure there won't be a problem finding him a good home. I'd take him myself but I've already got too many pets.'

'I can look after him for now.'

'Sure. I can sort you out with some food. Do you want to make a follow-up appointment at my clinic in a couple of days? I'm just a couple of suburbs away from here.' The look in Phoebe's eyes was one of admiration. 'I'm guessing you live near the air rescue base? You guys do such an awesome job...'

Nico wasn't about to confess that he was currently living in a camping ground that was quite a long way from his new job. Neither did he want to arrange a follow-up appointment that might give Phoebe the idea that he was interested in anything more than the only important thing on his mind right now, which was Bruce.

He'd never considered having a dog in his life before. He'd been far too busy with his career and making the most of any spare time travelling to discover the best beaches for surfing or paddleboarding and he loved the sometimes extended periods of living in his retro Volkswagen Kombi campervan, which offered no room for accommodating pets. He wasn't considering having a dog now either, but he'd assured Bruce he would look after him.

How could he not have made that promise? That look in the dog's eyes when he'd been holding him as they took off in the helicopter had been heartbreaking. More than heartbreaking, because Nico knew what it was like to have that little faith in the world.

To be at rock bottom and feel...total despair...

He'd held that eye contact with Bruce and, even before he'd said the words out loud, he'd known that the dog understood. That he was trusting him.

'I can give you a list of dog rescue shelters—just in case things don't work out.' Phoebe's glance was curious. 'Your job must mean some long shifts. That's not going to be a problem?'

'No.' Nico spoke with a confidence he was far from sure of. 'I don't think so. Thank you so much for your help. It will probably be only for a day or two and we'll be fine.'

The vet's bill was eye-watering, especially after Nico added some essentials like the food, a bowl, a brush and a blanket. He carried Bruce to his van and settled him on his own bed, before driving back to his grassy corner of the camping ground which was fortunately screened from the manager's office and residence by some thick hedges. Nico had no idea whether pets were allowed but Bruce wasn't about to go wandering with that sore leg and he'd be hidden from view when he drove in and out of the grounds. As long as he didn't start barking, his presence could remain secret for at least a few days.

Just between the two of them.

Like that feeling of connection that had already made it feel like they were a team.

When Nico finally edged into the noticeably depleted space on the mattress that filled most of the back of the van, he released his breath in a slightly resigned sigh. He only had a few hours now to grab some sleep before he was due back at work.

'It's the strangest first day anywhere,' he told Bruce.

Bruce was watching him carefully. Did he think that Nico was regretting bringing him home?

Nico touched the dog's head. 'It'll be okay,' he promised. 'Let's get some sleep.'

But Bruce's eyes were still open as Nico felt his own slowly shutting. He was almost asleep when he felt the soft warmth of the dog's body relaxing against his own. And then he felt the damp swipe of Bruce's tongue against his hand and it felt like gratitude.

Trust.

Love, even…?

Whatever it was, it felt like something that should not be broken.

It also felt like this was the end of a day when something even bigger than simply a new job had been started.

Something…important.

Sì… Nico felt himself drifting into a deep sleep with a hint of a smile curving his lips. This was *tutto bene*—all good. Maybe he'd found a door that had opened up a whole new life. If so, was he ready?

Yes. More than ready. He'd been keeping himself too busy to have time to think about some things for too long now. Maybe it was time he slowed down enough to take notice of the good things in life that had nothing to do with his work.

Frankie had, of course, noticed the bright red and white van parked in the SSAR base car park yesterday. Who wouldn't when it had surfboards tied to the roof rack and looked like it only needed some flowers painted on the sides to be a relic from the hippy era of the nineteen-sixties?

It wouldn't have occurred to her to associate something so unsophisticated with Nico Romano, however, until she arrived at work the next morning to find him standing beside the opened sliding door on the side. For a brief moment she was distracted by that rather fierce curling sensation in her gut that let her know exactly how attractive she found this man, and then she was startled by the realisation that all the men she'd ever dated in her life so far had had the streaked blond hair and sun-kissed skin of a dedicated Antipodean surfer. The only thing Nico had in common with any of them was the surfboard on top of this van and, for some reason, the idea that this was his chosen mode of transport was equally as startling.

'Is this *your* van?'

Nico's eyebrows rose at her tone. '*Sì*… Is it parked in the wrong place or something?'

'No… I just would have guessed that you'd drive something else.'

'Such as…?'

'Oh… I don't know…' Frankie was feeling slightly embarrassed now but it was too late to stop her mouth running away with her. 'A Lamborghini or a Ferrari, perhaps?'

'Why? Because I'm Italian?'

Frankie shrugged. 'Nah… Because you look kind of like you'd feel at home behind the wheel of a flashy sports car.'

He was wearing his uniform but hadn't tied his hair back yet and it was long enough for the curls to brush the collar of his dark blue shirt. It was glossy and black and looked as though it would be as soft as silk. She needed to stop looking at him right *now*, Frankie realised, but she also needed to avoid catching his gaze as she did so, because she definitely didn't want her new colleague to guess what she had just been thinking about. Or that brief fantasy he'd been included in on the way home from that job in Willhua last night. So she looked upwards.

'That's a weird sort of surfboard.'

'It's an SUP. A stand-up paddleboard.'

'Ah…of course it is.' Frankie cringed inwardly at saying something so ignorant. 'And that's something I've been meaning to try one day too. I love being near the sea and there's only so long you can keep swimming.' She was talking too much now, wasn't she? Frankie risked a quick glance to find Nico looking slightly bemused.

'So what do *you* drive, Frankie?'

'I don't drive. I ride. A Ducati. It's over

there, see?' She waved to where she'd parked her sleek black motorbike between a hangar and the main buildings.

'Because it's Italian?'

Frankie pretended to look shocked. 'Because it's the best bike on the road. Normally I would avoid anything Italian on principle.' She caught her bottom lip between her teeth. She didn't want to sound rude. And part of her didn't want to burn any bridges between herself and Nico before she was sure she didn't want to break her self-imposed rule. Or that the attraction to the total opposite of her normal 'type' wasn't simply a temporary aberration.

'Except for the food, of course...' she added. 'Nobody in their right mind would avoid Italian food, would they?'

'It's a good thing that there are so many good Italian restaurants in Australia,' Nico agreed. 'It will always be *my* favourite food.' He turned back to peer inside the van. 'And that reminds me, I'd better leave some food out for Bruce in case he gets hungry. He hasn't eaten anything yet.' He picked up a bag of kibble and shook some into a bowl, but he glanced up at Frankie as he did so. 'Why do you avoid everything Italian?'

He sounded genuinely curious but Frankie

pretended not to hear the question. 'Bruce is in your van?' She stepped closer. 'Hey...' She leaned in to pat the dog. 'Oh...his leg's bandaged. But not plastered. So it's not broken?'

'No. He may have torn ligaments and it's bruised badly enough for him to need to stay off it for a week or so. Which is good because he won't mind staying in the van to rest. Especially with the shade from these trees.'

'He certainly looks comfortable with that bed you've put in there for him. He's even got blankets and pillows.'

'Actually, it's my bed.'

Frankie blinked. Oh, my... Knowing that she was looking at Nico's bed had intensified that tingling sensation in her gut exponentially. What did he wear to sleep in? Or maybe he wore nothing at all...?

She cleared her throat hurriedly. 'I guess you need it for when you go camping. Or surfing?'

'I need it all the time at the moment. I haven't found a place to rent yet so I'm living at the camping ground over Bundeena way.'

'That's a bit of a drive to get to work.'

'Only forty-five minutes or so. Where do you live?'

'Lilli Pilli Point. It's a quick ride on the motorway to get to the base and, even better, about ten minutes' run from the reserve, so that's where I go every morning before work. Or after work so I can have a swim. There are some lovely saltwater swimming baths there.'

'Nice. What's the surf like there?'

Frankie laughed. 'There isn't any. There's a wharf and lots of boats moored offshore. There are some spots in the reserve where it's possible to get down to the sea but it's much easier to swim in the baths. You'll need to go to somewhere like Bondi if you want surf.'

Nico shook his head. 'Too many people,' he said. 'I prefer it quiet. And I don't need surf that often. Most of the time I prefer to paddleboard.'

Frankie gave Bruce a last scratch behind his ear. 'See you later,' she told the dog. 'I have to go to work now. In the helicopter. You had a ride in it yesterday, remember?'

Frankie certainly remembered. She could remember every detail of the entire day.

The day she'd met Mr Perfect.

The day she'd started to wonder if Nico might prove to be the exception to the rule she'd stuck to for so long.

'You've got food and water,' Nico said to Bruce. 'And the windows are open for some fresh air. And so that it doesn't smell too bad in here later. You kind of need a bath, mate. I'll come and let you out when we're not too busy, okay? And, after work, we could give you a bath. It's hot enough today and we can use the hose that Mozzie uses to wash the helicopter. You'd like that, wouldn't you?'

Frankie could see the way Bruce was listening to Nico. And the way his gaze was fixed on him as if he thought the world might end if Nico walked away. And now she was remembering the way Nico had been holding the dog last night and the way it had squeezed her heart so hard she could almost feel herself physically falling in love.

It was Bruce who'd given her a link with Nico already. This big, hairy, sad-looking dog that they'd both been involved in rescuing. Frankie had taken him to safety. Nico had taken him home.

'Why don't you bring him inside?' she suggested. 'Nobody would mind and even in the shade it might get too hot for him in the van.'

Nobody did mind having Bruce quietly sitting in a corner of the staffroom. Over the next few days everyone got used to seeing Nico taking responsibility for making sure the scruffy dog had food and water available at all times and carrying him outside to do his business on the grass by the car park when he was between jobs. It was even nicer to have him around after Nico had given him a soapy shower outside and spent most of an evening brushing tangles out of his long coat, but it was quickly apparent that, while Bruce was perfectly friendly and polite to anyone who paid him attention, Nico was his chosen person—the one he trusted in a confusing new world he'd found himself in.

Nico didn't mind that at all. He rather liked it, in fact.

'You could pretend that you like me, you know, mate.' Mozzie had crouched beside where Bruce was lying on his blanket to give him a scratch behind his ears, but the dog hadn't even wagged his tail in greeting. 'I was there too, when you were getting rescued.'

'So was I.' Frankie was making a mug of coffee. 'It was me who risked life and limb to get him off the cliff, remember?'

'Let's not make that too public,' Colin muttered as he walked past. 'Especially the bit about bringing him back to base.'

'Have you heard whether there are any relatives of the guy who died?' Ricky asked. 'People who want to take the dog?'

'Nothing,' Nico said. 'I rang the Willhua

cop again yesterday. He said he'd be in touch if they heard anything but for me not to hold my breath.'

'And I've spoken to Jenny,' Frankie said. 'She hasn't heard of any relatives or friends that are interested either. She's planning to adopt the other dog, Stumpy, if no one comes forward.'

'Stumpy?' Ricky was laughing. 'What kind of name for a dog is that?'

'He's a corgi, I believe. He's got short legs.'

'That's a terrible name.' Ricky shook his head. 'But no worse than Mozzie, I guess.'

'Why *are* you called Mozzie?' Nico asked.

'His real name is Murray.' Frankie was grinning now. 'He got the nickname because there's that annoying buzzing sound people can hear when he's getting close in his helicopter. Like the world's biggest mosquito.'

Mozzie was ignoring her. 'What will you do?' he asked Nico. 'If no one wants Bruce back?'

Nico hesitated. He hadn't thought that far ahead. What *would* he do? He turned his head, knowing perfectly well that he would find Bruce watching him. Even if the dog had his eyes shut and looked like he was sound asleep, Nico knew he only had to move an inch and he would be being watched again.

It was as if Bruce thought that if he didn't keep his eyes on him, Nico would vanish. At the same time, he was remembering the trust that had been placed in him. The way that being in physical contact with him had been enough to let an animal, that had to be very frightened and sore, relax enough to sleep. Already, that meant that handing Bruce to someone else—potentially a stranger who was only taking him from a sense of duty—was never going to feel right.

'I would keep him,' Nico said aloud. But then he frowned. 'But I would have to find somewhere else to live,' he said. 'I've seen a "No Dogs" sign at the camping ground and it's going to get harder to keep him hidden when he wants to walk.'

'You might have trouble finding somewhere to rent that lets you keep a pet.' Mozzie shrugged. 'I'd let you park on my lawn if I had one but all I have is a garage in the basement of my apartment block. Frankie… you've got a lawn, haven't you?'

'Yeah…and I also have a bunch of housemates who might have something to say about turning it into a caravan park.' Frankie ducked her head as though she was determined not to even look at Nico as she spoke.

'It's okay. I'll sort it.' Nico wanted this conversation to finish. He really didn't want to put Frankie on the spot. It felt like he was still waiting for her to make her mind up about accepting him as a colleague and he couldn't decide which way the balance was tipping.

On the negative side, she'd dropped comments like preferring to avoid anything Italian and that she thought he looked like someone who would show off his money by driving an expensive car. She also still seemed to be deliberately keeping her distance.

On the other side, though, there were moments when Nico felt something very different. When he caught her shifting her gaze as if she was disguising the fact she'd been watching him with at least interest, if not approval. Or when there was something about her body language that suggested she was not averse to being physically close to him. Was she actually having to force herself not to make eye contact right now?

Or, *oddio*…maybe that was wishful thinking?

Because, despite knowing that he would never allow any attraction to Frankie Moretti to come to anything, it was growing. Getting deeper as he noticed more and more things about her. Like her concern for Bruce being left in a vehicle that could become over-heated. How kind she had been with that confused elderly patient they had gone to yesterday. The way she lit up with the adren-aline rush of every new call. And how hot was it that she rode a motorbike?

Surely he had his life under control well enough now that being friends with Frankie wouldn't present a problem? Was it possible that he could enjoy the sensation of attrac-tion without it going any further?

'It's right over the road from the bush re-serve.'

'What? Sorry…' Nico blinked. 'What's that expression? I was…miles away…'

'Mmm…' There was a gleam of what looked like amusement in Frankie's dark eyes—as if she knew precisely in what di-rection he had just strayed. 'I was just say-ing that I've seen a "For Rent" sign on a place I run past on my way to the reserve. It's a hand-painted sign and it's been there for weeks, so it's either some mansion that's way too expensive for the market and the owners are too tight to pay for a proper sign, or it's so rundown it's uninhabitable, which is more likely. It's hidden by trees so I have no idea what it looks like.' Frankie reached for her pager as it sounded. 'Mind you, if it is rundown, the landlord probably wouldn't mind you having a dog. Might be worth having a look?'

'Absolutely.' Nico was reading the message on his own pager as more information came over their radios. Resources were being directed urgently to a serious traffic incident on a motorway involving a truck and several cars. He was on his feet by the time he finished reading the initial information but he turned to catch Frankie's gaze. 'After work?'

'Sure.' But Frankie's tone was offhand now. She was focused on the challenge ahead of them.

So was Nico, but as he took his seat in the helicopter and flipped his microphone down so he could communicate with his crewmates he couldn't resist a glance at Frankie's face. She didn't notice. She was focused on the screen of her tablet, gathering as much information as she could about what they were heading towards.

And Nico knew he might be in trouble if he didn't gain control very soon. Not simply because he was being distracted, if only for a heartbeat, from what he should be focused on, but because Frankie's passion for the work she did—that he understood so well it was automatically a deep connection between them—was just as sexy as everything else about this woman.

It was the kind of scene that road traffic management authorities dreaded. Multiple lanes of the major motorway leading into Australia's most populated city were blocked in both directions—by the accident on one side and, on the other, by the traffic slowing as people stared in horror at the carnage, causing a chain reaction of braking or even running into the back of other vehicles until all movement stopped.

Numerous police vehicles, fire trucks and ambulances were either on scene or fighting to get through the traffic jam but, fortunately, it was far enough out of the city for farmland to provide easy landing for more than one rescue helicopter. Mozzie stayed with the aircraft. Frankie, Nico and Ricky slipped backpacks on and picked up other gear like a defibrillator and suction unit. They headed for what looked a triage area that had been established near a police command vehicle and found an ambulance scene commander updating a whiteboard with the number of patients and the status of their condition.

'We've got the fire service extracting a category two patient with a spinal injury. He's got a paramedic with him who's keeping him immobilised. The driver of that vehicle is category zero. We've got two category threes in the back of an ambulance that's about to transport them and some non-urgent minor injuries that are still being assessed.' He indicated the area behind him in the triage tent where several people were seated and being attended to.

'We can leave our crewman, Ricky, here to help with that until we know where we'll be most useful,' Frankie said.

'Thanks. There's a category one with a head injury currently being loaded into the other chopper but where we need you guys is over there...' He pointed to a cluster of people almost hidden by the truck trailer that was leaning at an ominous angle. 'There was a motorbike that got caught up in the middle of this mess. Young guy who's conscious but the crew with him has just upgraded him from a category three to a two. His blood pressure's dropping.'

Frankie nodded. The lower the category number, the more serious condition the patient was in. This patient had been initially assessed as someone who had a potentially life-threatening condition and needed treatment within thirty minutes to someone with an imminently life-threating condition who needed treatment within ten minutes. The category one who was in the helicopter lifting off the ground as Frankie and Nico went towards the truck was critically ill or in cardiac arrest and a category zero was dead.

Nico increased his pace to step sideways in front of Frankie but she had to slow down to not bump into him and she could feel herself frowning. Why was he changing direction to walk away from the patient they were about to reach?

'Hey…' Nico's call was loud enough to attract the attention of a fire officer who was watching his crew using pneumatic cutting gear to get into a car. Frankie could see a paramedic in the back seat of the vehicle, holding the front passenger's head still, under a plastic sheet to protect both himself and the patient in the front seat from shattering glass.

'What's up, buddy?'

'How stable is this truck trailer? And are there any dangerous goods inside it?'

'It's a load from a grocery warehouse. No chemicals. And it's been checked. It's not about to tip over on you lot.'

Nico nodded. He was looking up as he moved forward again. Scanning for potential hazards like a damaged power line?

Frankie realised she'd almost made a rookie mistake of assuming that the crew already there would have cleared the scene for hazards. Nico was being cautious but he was alert to anything that could put them in danger. He was doing his best to keep her safe and Frankie's level of trust in her partner just went up a notch. He had her back. At another time she might well have his, if he forgot a step in a protocol or found himself needing assistance with a procedure.

Because that was what partners did. In a good partnership they not only filled any gaps in the other's performance but they enabled each other to do better than they could have done on their own.

Working with Jenny had been great but Frankie knew, deep down, that working with Nico already had the potential to be even better. More challenging.

More satisfying.

She took a deep breath as they arrived beside a man lying on the gravel of the motorway verge, having his clothing cut clear of his legs by two ambulance officers that looked young enough to be new on the job. Both legs were lying in an odd position with the feet turned outwards.

'Bilateral external rotation,' Frankie said

quietly to Nico as she slipped off the straps of her backpack.

'But no obvious deformation from fractures.'

They shared a glance. They knew that this patient's condition had deteriorated due to a falling blood pressure and the most likely cause for that in this situation was blood loss. Internal, because there was no sign of blood on the road or his clothing. And the most likely cause of that blood loss, given the way his legs were lying, was a fractured pelvis—an injury that could potentially be fatal within a short period of time.

'Hiya...' Frankie crouched near the head of a very pale young man whose helmet had already been removed. 'My name's Frankie and I've got Nico with me. We're going to help the crew here to get you sorted and then we're going to get you into hospital just as quickly as we can. Is that okay with you?'

He gave a single nod. 'It hurts...'

'The whistle isn't helping enough?' Frankie could see he was clutching a 'green whistle' which delivered the pain-relieving drug Methoxyflurane.

'No...'

'We'll do something about that very soon. I just need to find out a bit more about you.'

Frankie put a hand on his wrist to check for a radial pulse, but looked up to find the junior paramedics looking relieved. 'Tell me what you've found so far,' she invited.

She had time to collect any information on the latest vital signs that had been recorded because, in her peripheral vision, she could see that Nico had also noticed that no IV access had been obtained. He was collecting everything he needed to put a line in, administer effective pain relief and get some fluids running to try and stabilise the blood pressure. He had located the pelvic splint pack as well so they could slip the belt around the injured biker's hips and tighten it enough to keep the pelvis stable and hopefully control any internal blood loss.

Frankie felt the stress levels, that were always there in this first assessment of a potentially critically injured patient, easing in a way that meant they were not about to undermine her confidence in the job she was about to do. With a noticeable—and welcome—shift, she felt a new kind of confidence in what she was capable of doing, knowing that she had someone like Nico working with her. Backing her up.

Keeping her safe. Again…

CHAPTER FOUR

THE ORIGIN OF the piece of wood at the end of the driveway that had the words 'For Rent' and a mobile phone number painted on it became obvious as Frankie and Nico got far enough to see what lay behind the trees.

The ancient beach house was falling apart and the plank of wood that had been used for the sign had no doubt once been part of the collapsed garden shed or car port near the house. The paint peeling off the sides of the house was pale blue and it was a simple box shape of a square window on either side of a front door, like a child's drawing. The corrugated iron roof was rusty and the veranda sagged in the middle but when they ventured cautiously up the steps to peer through the grimy glass of the windows, the boards of the veranda felt sturdy enough and the empty room looked intact and, more importantly, weatherproof.

And when they turned back and caught a glimpse of the sea through the small forest of gum tree trunks, with the pink glow of a sunset just beginning, they both caught a breath.

'Oh…wow…' Frankie murmured. 'Nico… this is gorgeous.' Her breath escaped in a huff of laughter. 'Apart from the house, of course.'

But when they were walking away and she took another glance over her shoulder at this little dwelling, Frankie's imagination was captured. She could see it renovated. Freshly painted, with white wicker chairs on the veranda. The front door was open and she could imagine the laughter of excited children getting ready to run down to the reserve to play or to go to the pool for a swim. She could imagine living in this house. With her own family. Sitting on that veranda, watching the sun going down, with the father of those children sitting beside her, holding her hand…

A man who had dark hair and even darker eyes? Like Nico?

It would be…

Well…perfect. Like any good fantasy.

Without any basis in reality at all, of course, which was why it was a fantasy. She really had to stop having daydreams like this, but they'd been happening almost ever since she'd first been aware of her attraction to Nico. If they got any worse they could be a threat to their working relationship but, fortunately, this particular bubble of that flight of fancy vanished almost as soon as it had appeared. Nico hadn't even noticed that Frankie was momentarily distracted as he paused to follow the direction of her gaze.

'I would need to see more inside,' he said. 'And find out if it has running water and electricity. Or maybe that doesn't matter so much. If it's not too expensive. It might work for now, even if it was just a place to park my van without the rules of a camping ground about dogs. I could swim in the sea to shower if I had to. And I have somewhere to cook already with my gas stove.'

'Oh, no…' Frankie's eyes widened. 'It's Friday, isn't it?'

'Ah…yes…' Nico lifted an eyebrow. 'Do you have somewhere you need to be?'

Frankie nodded. 'Home. We have a thing in our share house where we all take a turn to cook on a Friday night and everyone who isn't working comes home for dinner. You talking about cooking just reminded me that it's my turn.' She turned away from the view. She even walked a few steps away from Nico but then she turned her head. 'You're welcome to come. I always make way too much food. We never quite know who's coming or bringing someone home with them.'

'Ah...no... I need to look after Bruce. Maybe I will take him down to see the reserve. A soak in seawater might be good for his leg.'

'He's welcome too.'

Suddenly—for a reason Frankie had no intention of trying to analyse—she really wanted to cook for Nico. Italian food. 'I'm making pasta *alla gricia*,' she told him.

Nico looked as if she'd just cast a magic spell on him. 'How did you know?' he demanded.

'Know what?'

'That it's my absolute favourite.' He licked his lips. 'Do you use spaghetti or *rigatori*?'

'*Rigatori*, of course. I'd make my own but the shop I go to for the *guanciale* makes fresh pasta every day. And they deliver. There will be a box of ingredients on my doorstep, which is only five minutes' drive away from here.' Frankie offered Nico a smile as she raised her eyebrows. 'Are you sure I can't tempt you?'

Oh...my... The smouldering look in Nico's eyes, that looked completely black in this fading light, made Frankie's heart skip a beat and then race to catch up as she recognised the *double entendre* she had inadvertently delivered. Would he look like this if she was trying to tempt him to do something quite different than eating her homecooked food? She had to clear her throat as she cut the eye contact. It had already gone on too long.

'I mean…we've survived this week working together and we have our days off starting tomorrow. That's something to celebrate, isn't it? If I know my housemates, there'll be a stack of cold beers in the fridge and… hey…why don't you take a photo of the sign at the end of the drive and you can ring the owner. You might even be able to arrange to look inside the place while you're on this side of the bay and it could save you a long drive tomorrow.'

Nico raised his hands in a gesture of surrender as he walked towards her. Frankie began heading down the driveway again as if this was no big deal, but he caught up with her in a few long strides. He tipped his head towards her and she could hear the smile in his voice. His lips were close enough to her ear to be almost able to *feel* his voice—in a shiver that went straight to Frankie's bones.

'You had me at pasta *alla gricia*,' he said.

* * *

Frankie found herself feeling very uncharacteristically nervous during that five-minute ride home with Nico following her in his van.

Inviting Nico to dinner was not exactly keeping a professional distance and, even though the jury might have resoundingly offered the verdict that he was going to more than fit in with the rest of the crew on Red Watch, there was still that personal judgement that Frankie was struggling with.

Or, if she was honest, that personal *attraction* that was giving her grief.

Part of her—something that was probably being directed by her body rather than her brain—was rather hoping that all her housemates had taken on extra shifts at their workplaces or had received offers they couldn't refuse, like free tickets to some not-to-be-missed rock concert or something, because that would mean it would be just her and Nico.

Alone. Cooking and eating the food they both loved. Cementing another connection thanks to a shared heritage.

The part of her that was under instruction from her brain, however, was very relieved to find that everybody was at home or on their way. She left Nico in his van to get changed out of his uniform and grabbed the clothes that were lying on the end of her bed so that she didn't give herself time to even think about putting on something—like a dress—that would make her housemates think this was anything more than simply inviting a new colleague for dinner. She was in her denim cut-offs with a soft top that was knotted at the hem on one side and hadn't bothered putting anything on her feet, when Nico came in wearing a pair of black jeans and a tee shirt that was so ancient the image of the Italian flag on the front was cracked and faded. This was good, Frankie decided. Ordinary clothes. She had that tingle well under control.

Until she looked down to see Bruce approaching, carefully using only three legs, and noticed that Nico, like herself, had bare feet and, oh, boy...that tingle had moved to a whole new level. It was more like a spear of sensation, centred deep in her belly but firing outwards so fast it had reached her toes before she could blink. A sensation that was actually painful but in a rather delicious way.

To avoid thinking that she might be in a spot of trouble as far as staying firmly in control of her attraction to Nico, Frankie took the box of ingredients that had been put on the kitchen table to the bench. She opened cupboards then, to find the enormous pot she used to cook pasta and another one for making the sauce. Then she collected a chopping board, sharp knife and grater, just throwing an occasional smile over her shoulder, casually introducing everyone to each other as the housemates gathered in this large kitchen area.

'Nico, this is Justin—he's a paramedic based in Miranda and that's his girlfriend Janine. Guys, this is Nico and that's Bruce. I told you about rescuing him off the cliff the other night, didn't I?'

Suzie, a theatre nurse at St Mary's, was already on the floor giving Bruce some love when the final housemate, Derek, arrived home and headed straight for the fridge.

'What a day,' he said. 'Who else wants a beer?'

The enthusiastic chorus of assent suggested that Nico had instantly become a part of this group of friendly, intelligent people that he had plenty in common with. He even recognised Derek.

'I've seen you somewhere before, haven't I?'

'On the roof of St Mary's.' Derek nodded. 'When you brought that guy in who'd broken his ankle and then had a cardiac arrest on the way back.'

Nico nodded as he accepted the icy-cold lager with a wedge of lime stuffed into the neck of the bottle. 'Of course...you don't know what happened to him, do you?'

'He went to the Cath lab, got three stents and got discharged with minimal myocardial damage, I believe. He went home with a cast on his leg, a pair of crutches and some advice about lifestyle changes. You did a good job.' Derek made a face. 'Don't get the wrong idea—I don't normally stalk everyone who comes through our department but I know how much Frankie appreciates a follow-up.'

'I do,' Frankie agreed. 'And I appreciate my friends working in the right places.' She was slicing up the *guanciale* with its stripe of pink meat between layers of fat, putting it into a saucepan to render over a low heat.

'That smells *so* good.' Suzie got up to peer over Frankie's shoulder. 'What is it? Salami? Pancetta?' She threw a glance at Nico. 'We love it when it's Frankie's turn to cook.'

'It's a type of salami made from pig cheeks,' Frankie said. 'It's stronger than pancetta. Spiced with black pepper and chilli.'

Nico had moved closer as well. 'And that's *Pecorino Romano*.'

'Stinky cheese,' Justin declared. 'We've had that before. It's made from sheep's milk, isn't it?'

'Oh, gross...' Janine made a face. 'Don't tell me anything else.'

'You'll love it,' Nico assured her. 'But if you don't, I can help. It's the favourite thing my *nonna* used to cook for us when I was a kid.'

'What part of Italy do you come from, Nico?' Suzie asked. 'And what made you come to Sydney?'

'What made you want to work with Frankie?' Derek shook his head. 'Did no one warn you how bossy she can be?'

'Hey...' Frankie lifted her hand in protest, still holding her sharp knife. 'I'm the one slaving over a hot stove, here.'

Everyone noticed the way that Nico stiffened and took a swift step backwards as if he was feigning horror. Bruce had to hop, keeping his injured leg off the floor, but he was at Nico's side instantly, his alarmed gaze fixed on Frankie.

There was a shout of laughter in the room. 'She might be bossy,' Derek said, 'but she's quite safe with knives.'

'As far as we know,' Justin offered.

Nico looked embarrassed now. Frankie put

the knife down and focused on her cooking but there was still a beat of something awkward in the room. Instinct suggested that there had been something more than the pretence of fear in Nico's eyes. Had he found himself in a situation when he'd been under threat, perhaps? When he'd been truly afraid?

Maybe that thought could have undermined the sheer masculinity of the man but, instead, the hint of something softer—as compelling as vulnerability, perhaps—only drew Frankie towards him on a different but no less powerful level. The urge to offer protection felt like a physical squeeze on her heart.

'Come outside,' Suzie suggested. 'It's cooler under the tree. We can drag some bean chairs from the lounge onto the lawn and have dinner out there.'

It was one of those great nights that had an alchemy to make it something special. The solar fairy lights wound through the branches of the big tree on the lawn were shining and there was a contented silence as everyone tucked into the bowls of steaming, fragrant pasta.

She was watching Nico as he took his first bite and caught her breath as she watched him close his eyes with the pleasure of filling his mouth with that *al dente* pasta in its simple creamy sauce of spicy meat and cheese. Food that *she* had cooked. And then he licked some sauce off his lips with his eyes still closed and Frankie found her glow of pride being overtaken by sheer physical desire. There was something else in that mix as well. Something nice that came from providing food. Caring for someone… Something that was on the same level as knowing that someone could be vulnerable? Being able to nurture as well as protect?

By the time they'd all eaten their fill of the delicious meal Frankie had created, Nico was definitely part of the group. They all had the common interest of working in the medical world and it was easy to swap stories they could all appreciate. When it degenerated into a competition of who had seen the case of the strangest foreign objects people had swallowed they were in fits of laughter.

'Teeth,' Derek told them. 'Three of them.'

'Well, three is a little excessive,' Justin agreed. 'But it's not that unusual to swallow a tooth.'

'These weren't his own,' Derek said.

'Oops…' Frankie was lying on the grass, enjoying the fairy lights above her. She propped herself up on one elbow when Nico offered a story.

'I did my paramedic training in Milan,' he told them, 'and, I kid you not, one of the jobs on my very first day on the road was somebody who had swallowed the remote control for the television. He'd been having an argument with his wife about what programme to watch. When we arrived, she was trying to punch him in the stomach to change the channel. He was so drunk he thought it was funny.'

Frankie thought it was funny too, but she was only smiling rather than laughing aloud.

Because it was dark enough for nobody to notice that her gaze was lingering on Nico and her mind had gone wandering again. She loved this kind of social occasion. Being in a group of people. Being in a couple within that group was even better, because when it broke up you still weren't alone.

Frankie had been brought up in a big Italian community in Melbourne but she'd been an only child, because her mother had never remarried after her father died. She'd been far more inclined to be out on the streets trying to join in the boys' games of football than to be inside her own house and she'd watched in envy as extended families celebrated the arrival of every new baby. It had felt like she was the only one without siblings and that was when the seeds of her plan to create a big family of her own one day were planted.

Not having a father wasn't as bad as not having siblings because she was showered with love from her mother and grandmother and even at a young age she could see that the males were dominant enough in her community to be intimidating. The children were disciplined, sometimes strictly, and the women were mostly expected to adhere to the traditional roles of caring for the children, keeping house and cooking the food. When the local boys who wanted nothing more than to be seen as 'Italian stallions' assumed Frankie would like nothing more than to date them and, one day, marry one of them, the seeds of rebellion had really been sown. Francesca Moretti was going to be her own woman and forge her own destiny.

It didn't mean she didn't want a whole bunch of kids, mind you—enough that they would never be lonely—but it would be with someone who would be an equal partner. Even the painful wakes of broken relationships hadn't been enough to dent the dream of creating that big, loving family.

A family that would always gather to share

food like they were doing tonight, to celebrate every good thing in life but also gather
to offer comfort for the not so good things.
She was thirty-four years old and she still
hadn't found the relationship that was even
close to a foundation strong enough to build
a family on.

'Who wants coffee?' Derek asked. 'I'll
make it.'

'I'll help.' Nico got up when everyone
agreed that it would make a good end to the
dinner. He also helped to collect the empty
bowls and used cutlery and Frankie held hers
up as he came her way.

'Thank you. It's Brownie points if you do
the dishes around here.'

'Of course,' Nico said. 'You cooked, you
don't get to clean up. But it's me who should
be thanking *you*.' He was smiling down at
her. '*Grazie mille*, Frankie.' He gave a chef's
kiss. '*È stato delizioso.*'

Maybe it was hearing him speak in the lilt-
ing language of her heritage. Or that they'd
been eating the kind of food that was uniquely
Italian and how much Nico had loved it had
made her feel so proud. So…happy.

Or perhaps it was because she'd just been
thinking of family and children and the
yearning to fill in the gaps of what had been

missing in her own childhood. Quite possibly, it was as simple as watching the most attractive man she'd ever met in her life walking away with his hands full of dirty dishes.

Whatever it was, her black and white rules were getting smudged into an increasingly indistinct greyness. The rule about never dating Italian men, for one. Even the one about never dating someone she was working closely with might not be as ironclad as she'd thought.

By the time Nico was back and they were all sipping coffee and polishing off a box of chocolates Suzie had contributed, Frankie was almost ready to make a momentous decision.

She was actually prepared to break yet another one of her rules. The lesser known rule about not being the one to ask someone out on a date. Nobody would ever guess that the confidence Frankie could display in every other aspect of her life was totally lacking when it came to feeling desirable. She'd been discarded in favour of other women too many times by those blond, blue-eyed Aussie surfer dudes. Even the one she'd been in such a long-term relationship with she had been sure that he would end up being the father of her children.

But… Nico was different. And, being Italian, he probably wanted children as much as she did. She knew he was older than her by a few years. The timing could be as perfect as everything else.

Maybe the stars were finally aligning themselves.

Or was it another fantasy that she might have found the 'one'? The holy grail of romance that was too big to be bound by any rules.

It was too good to be true, of course, but then Frankie remembered that smouldering look when she'd asked if she could tempt him and she knew she had to find the courage to at least try and find out or she might regret it for ever.

Bruce was now lying on the lawn beside him, his head on Nico's knee, looking up at him as his ears were being softly rubbed.

'He knows you rescued him,' Suzie said. 'He adores you, doesn't he?'

'We belong together,' Nico said. 'I never knew it was a dog that was missing from my life, you know?'

Justin laughed. 'You've got yourself a fur kid.'

'A what?' Nico seemed to be unfamiliar with the expression.

'It's what people call their pets when they're substitute children,' Derek explained. 'They're the chosen kids but they're covered in fur.'

'You can have both,' Frankie put in. 'The best families have real kids *and* a dog.'

'Dogs are so much easier.' Justin was laughing. 'You can leave them home alone when you want to go out and have a good time. They kind of frown on you doing that with the human kids.'

'True…' Nico nodded. 'Another good reason why a fur kid is certainly the only sort of child I will ever have.'

Frankie blinked. This wasn't a part of the script for her perfect fantasy coming to life. 'You don't want real kids?'

'Not on my own, no…'

Frankie focused on the mug of coffee in her hand but didn't drink any because she was holding her breath. Waiting for someone else to break the silence?

Suzie obliged. 'No problem. You just need to find the person who wants a real kid as well as a fur kid.'

'A wife?' Nico's voice was quiet. 'No, thank you. Been there, done that.' His next quiet words that almost sounded like he was thinking aloud fell into a new, slightly shocked silence. *'Il gatto scottato teme l'acqua fredda.'*

'Huh?' Janine was staring at him. 'What does that mean?'

It was Frankie who translated. 'Literally, it means the scalded cat fears cold water.'

It felt remarkably as if she had just been doused in icy cold water herself. Or maybe it was more like being hit with something much more solid, because she was experiencing the sensation of being completely crushed. Derek was still looking bemused.

'The equivalent in English would probably be once bitten, twice shy,' she added.

And, in this context, someone whose marriage had been so bad it would never happen again.

'Ah…' The murmur from more than one person was sympathetic.

'You just need to find the right woman, mate,' Justin said. He smiled at Janine. 'That can change everything.'

Nico was also smiling but he was shaking his head. 'It's time I took my fur child home,' he said. 'Thank you all very much for having me. If I end up living down the road, I will return the invitation.' He lifted a hand in Frankie's direction. 'Enjoy your days off,' he said. 'I'll see you at work again next week.'

At work.

As a colleague.

And that was all Nico was ever going to be, despite any brave ideas on Frankie's part to ask him out.

She had heard the undertone in Nico's voice when he'd muttered that expression in his first language. There had been an indisputable finality about his words when he said he had no desire to repeat what had clearly been a disastrous marriage. That he had no desire to have human children either.

Which meant that the only kind of relationship Nico would want would be a no-strings 'friends with benefits' kind of arrangement and that was not something Frankie would ever choose. Not at this stage in her life, anyway. It hadn't mattered so much a decade ago, but it was probably what too many past boyfriends had assumed they had with her so it had been all too easy for them to move on and Frankie's heart had been broken too often. She didn't have any more time to waste on dead ends. She needed more in her life.

She needed a family.

But Nico Romano was not going to be the man to be a part of that dream.

And that was quite astonishingly disappointing. Weirdly, it felt almost as heartbreaking as she remembered the failure of actual romances to have been.

No. It was more than weird. It was ridiculous. As Frankie watched Nico's van disappear into the night, she made a new vow. She had four days off and she was going to use every one of them to push a 'reset' button. By the time she was back at work she might even be ready to laugh at herself for the stupid fantasies she'd been having about a new colleague.

She had to get over it, didn't she? Frankie wasn't about to follow her friend Jenny's example and hide away in some sleepy little country town to escape. No.

Nico had the right idea about such challenges in life. The way through this was to keep herself too busy to have time to think about it.

CHAPTER FIVE

FRANKIE WAS NOT HAPPY.

Everything had seemed normal when Nico had arrived back at the South Sydney Air Rescue base this morning. She'd even looked pleased to hear his news that he had signed a lease for the beach house property in her neighbourhood.

'It has electricity. A bathroom, even. No furniture, but I won't need much.'

'Have you been online?' Frankie asked. 'You should find everything you need for next to nothing there.'

'*Sì…*' Nico had already been online to search the most popular digital marketplace. 'I have already picked up a fridge. When I find the extra kitchen things, I'll be able to make dinner for you and your housemates. I enjoyed Friday night a lot.'

Frankie smiled but her gaze slid away from his almost instantly. 'You don't need to do that,' she said. 'And it's pretty difficult to get us all in the same place on the same night. Friday was a bit of a fluke.'

Nico frowned. He could sense something wasn't quite right. Was it because he wasn't understanding well enough?

'A fluke? Isn't that a musical instrument?'

'That's a *flute*.'

This time, when Frankie smiled, Nico knew what had felt wrong. This smile was genuine, not simply polite. And…it was a gorgeous smile. He could actually *feel* it as much as he could see it. In his gut somewhere. Or perhaps it was in his heart.

'A fluke is something that happens by luck rather than good management,' Frankie was explaining. 'A *colpo di fortuna*, perhaps? Sorry, my Italian is very rusty. It's obviously time I went home to visit my *nonna*.'

She'd understood well enough to translate the saying about the scalded cat that he hadn't actually meant to say aloud the other night, but Nico was still processing the fact that she had initially given him a smile that was polite enough to be distant. Impersonal.

It shouldn't bother him. But it did. It was how Frankie had been around him when he'd first arrived. Before they'd worked together long enough to know they could trust each other professionally. Before she'd cooked that amazing meal and he'd sat under a tree with fairy lights through its branches amidst the laughter of people who had happily included him as part of their group. An evening where Nico had felt more like he could simply be himself than he could remember feeling safe to be in such a long time it felt like for ever.

He tried to shrug off the setback. It shouldn't matter if they weren't going to be good friends.

Except it did.

He liked Frankie.

He *really* liked her. He would very much like to be part of her circle of friends. He wanted to be able to be in her company away from work and share a meal again. To hear her laughter and get to know her. She was an Australian-born Italian but how similar were their backgrounds? Was she as close to her *nonna* as he had been to his? Did she have a big, noisy, nosy family like he did? Was he going to make Frankie even less happy if he asked a personal question or two? It was worth finding out.

'Where's home?' he asked.

'Melbourne.'

'And that's where your whole family lives?'

'Just my *nonna*. And my mother.' Frankie

shrugged. 'But that is my whole family, yes. My father died when I was too young to remember so my mother moved back to be with *her* mother.'

'No brothers or sisters?'

'Nope.' The word was clipped and Nico got the impression that was the end of the conversation. It was his turn to shrug. 'Maybe you were lucky,' he told her. 'I have four sisters and they were always fighting with each other.'

She only looked directly at him for a split-second but it was enough for Nico to see something in Frankie's eyes that was...what was it? Sadness? Had he stumbled on something private, like a past tragedy in her family? Nico knew about how important it could be to keep some things private. He opened his mouth to apologise for telling her she was lucky not to have brothers or sisters, but Frankie was making a sound that was vaguely dismissive and then she wandered away to stare out of the huge windows that overlooked the helipad. Mozzie and Ricky were busy with the aircraft. Going through an equipment checklist, perhaps?

Was Frankie creating distance in the hope that he wouldn't ask her any more personal questions? Wishing for a call-out that would put them into a professional space that would make it totally inappropriate to pry into her private life?

If so, she got her wish. Nico could feel his pager vibrating on his belt and the sharp tone of its beeping. At the same time, Colin's voice came through the loudspeaker system.

'Tango Papa Bravo. Code One. Two-vehicle MVA on the M31, vicinity of Yanderra. GPS coordinates coming through. Police and ambulance in attendance.'

Frankie was already heading through the door on the way downstairs to the helipad. She hadn't waited to hold it open for Nico.

It kind of looked like she was running away from him.

And the fact that it bothered him this much was a warning that he knew he needed to take heed of.

He could do the distant thing as well as she could if that was what it was going to take to make her feel safe enough to drop her defences.

Motor vehicle accidents were an almost routine deployment for Air Rescue, especially when they were in semi-rural areas with a long transport time to a hospital that had major trauma capability and on motorways with their higher speed limits that meant that collisions were much more likely to involve serious injuries.

Seeing the dents in a car roof that indicated the vehicle had rolled and that the engine of the second car was lying in the centre of a motorway lane were early indications that the mechanism of injury was significant so the victims had a high chance of serious injuries. There was an ambulance, a rapid response vehicle, police and fire service personnel on scene.

Frankie knew the critical care paramedic who'd arrived on scene in his rapid response vehicle and was currently kneeling at the head of a female patient, lying on the ground beside the car that had been sideswiped with such ferocity it had lost its engine and a front wheel.

'Hey, Tom.' Frankie crouched beside him. 'This is the patient you've called rapid transport for, yes?'

Tom nodded. 'I've just intubated her to protect her airway.' He squeezed the bag in his hand, watching the chest rise. 'She was unconscious on arrival with a GCS of three. Airbags were deployed but I'm thinking there must have been something loose that hit her head. She's got unequal pupils, bleeding from her ears and this bruising coming up around her eyes suggests a basal skull fracture. She's also got a widening pulse pressure so the sooner she gets to ED the better. A ten-minute flight time is a hell of a lot better than at least forty-five minutes by road.'

'Let's load and go, then. We'll get her hooked up to our portable ventilator as soon as we get her onboard.' Frankie looked up to signal Ricky that the scoop stretcher was needed. Behind him, she could see Nico kneeling in front of a small girl who was sitting on the lowered back steps of the ambulance. She was holding a doll in one hand and was crying. Frankie swallowed hard. 'There were children in the car?'

'Just the one,' Tom told her. 'Her name's Amelia and she's nearly four years old. She was in a good quality car seat in the back and appears uninjured, but if you've got room to take her with her mum that would be ideal. Nobody's been able to contact the dad yet.'

'We can do that.' Frankie nodded.

'Great. When they find Dad, they can send him straight to St Mary's. We haven't told Amelia how badly hurt Mum might be. She thinks she's just having a bit of a sleep because she's tired.'

'What about the other vehicle involved?' Frankie had more than enough medical assistance with the patient she'd headed for, but had Nico been right to stop to talk with a child who was already with a ground crew paramedic rather than going to the vehicle that had flipped?

'Teenage driver.' Tom blew out a huff of breath. 'Extricated himself and appears okay. He's refused medical attention, probably due to his alcohol level. Must have been some night last night, that's all I can say. The police are dealing with him.'

Ricky had separated the two sections of the scoop stretcher. Tom continued to look after the airway and breathing for their patient as Frankie helped a paramedic log roll her just enough to slide one section beneath her body. She pushed aside clothing that had already been cut and ran her hand down the spine before they lowered her onto the stretcher.

'No obvious spinal injury.'

They repeated the process on the other side, clicked the scoop stretcher together and lifted it onto the air mattress on top of the helicopter stretcher. Ricky placed the padded blocks on either side of the patient's head, ready to tape them into position to add extra immobilisation.

'Loosen the collar as soon as that's taped,' Frankie reminded him. 'And we want a slight thirty-degree up-tilt on her head to improved venous drainage.'

Another sideways glance revealed Nico still with the child. It looked like he was simply talking to Amelia but Frankie was quite confident that he would be doing another assessment of whether or not she was injured. He'd be watching and listening to any signs or symptoms that her breathing might be affected, looking at skin colour and any obvious bruising, listening to her speech to see how oriented and alert she was and, even though it was usually the quietest children who had the most serious injuries, that crying could be due to significant pain.

Nico's face did look as if he'd found out something very concerning but, as she and Ricky got closer with the stretcher, Frankie could see that the little girl was only holding the body of her fashion doll in one hand with nothing more than a plastic bobble on top of its neck. In her other hand she was holding a head with improbably long, curly blonde hair and the little girl looked distraught. Nico looked up and nodded as he registered that they were on the move to load and go as soon as possible.

'Is Amelia coming with us?'

'Yes.'

'Come on, *cara*. Let's go with Mummy.'

'But I want you…to fix Princess Pixie,' Amelia wailed.

'The hospital is the best place for anyone who has hurt their head,' Nico said. 'For mummies and princesses. But you know what?'

'What?'

'I might be able to operate on Princess Pixie on the way.' Nico held out his hand and Frankie watched as Amelia didn't hesitate to respond. She held up her arms, her face still crumpled in grief for her beloved doll, no doubt mixed with shock from the accident and confusion and fear for her mother. Nico scooped the child up and she buried her face against his neck as he strode alongside the stretcher.

And Frankie looked at those small arms wound around Nico's neck and the cloud of still baby-soft hair covering the head snuggled against his shoulder and her heart just melted.

Did he have any idea what a wonderful father he could be? He clearly had the gift of winning a frightened child's trust and Frankie knew how hard that could be. Children—and dogs, for that matter—had an intuition about people and Nico was one of the good guys. It was kind of heartbreaking if a bad marriage had put him off ever creating a family of his own.

But it was none of Frankie's business and allowing her heart to be melted was not helping her consolidate the new boundaries she had put in place in the last few days to prevent the possibility of stepping anywhere near that dead end street on a relationship map. Being in the friend zone didn't include getting misty-eyed over seeing a man being so charming to a small child.

She focused completely on monitoring Amelia's mother on the short flight to St Mary's and their patient was stable enough for her not to need assistance for the moment, which meant that both Nico and Ricky had the chance to look after Amelia. A glance behind her showed Nico lifting one side of the headphones Amelia was wearing so she could hear him over the noise of the rotors. Frankie could hear what he was saying through the headphones in her helmet.

'Can you give me the head, please, Nurse Amelia? I think I'm ready for the reattachment surgery. There…'

Frankie glanced behind her to see Nico pushing the doll's head back onto the bobble.

'*Va meglio*… That's better. As good as new…'

A chuckle of laughter came from Ricky. 'First successful recapitation I've seen. Good job, team.'

'I think she needs a bandage,' Nico said. 'What do you think, Nurse Amelia?'

'Mummy gives me a sticky plaster when I get an ouch.' Amelia was sitting so close to Nico that Frankie could hear her voice via Nico's microphone.

'Ricky?' There was suppressed laughter in Nico's voice. 'Do we happen to have a sticky plaster for ouches in our supplies?'

'I think I can probably find one.'

So the handover on the roof of St Mary's involved not only a human with a head injury but a doll who had enough of a bandage around its neck to look like it was also wearing a cervical collar. When Frankie saw Amelia looking over the shoulder of the nurse who was carrying her in the wake of her mother's stretcher, so that she could keep her gaze fixed on Nico, she knew she was going to have to work a bit harder on those boundaries.

What was it about men who were gentle with children or loved their dogs that was so sexy? Was it because it suggested that they would also look after the woman in their life with the same level of care? Physical sex appeal was one thing but passion with a background of an ability to care—and protect—was a whole different planet of attractiveness.

Mr Perfect was making it a lot harder than she had anticipated to get over her attraction.

Hot, humid end-of-summer nights made it harder to sleep.

Lying awake made it harder not to think about Nico.

It was, however, getting easier to work with him as they began their next four-day roster together on Red Watch. Nico was settling in, both to his new house and his new job. Bruce was also settling into his new life. He came to work with Nico and lay quietly in a corner of the staff area or a hangar or under the table at mealtimes. The dog's leg was healing well, although he was still walking with a limp and had perfected the cute trick of holding his front paw up as if it was hurting when he wanted attention from Nico.

'Have you heard yet whether there's any family who might want to take Bruce on?' Frankie hadn't missed the way Nico was sharing his lunch by slipping scraps of food under the table to Bruce.

'No.' Nico was fondling Bruce's ear now. 'I think I'm afraid to ask. I would miss him very much if someone comes forward.'

'I could ask Jen,' Frankie offered. 'I imagine she's feeling the same way about Stumpy by now.'

'Maybe it wasn't a new life she needed at all,' Mozzie put in. 'Maybe she just needed a dog in her life instead of dating a bastard.' He glanced up. 'Who are *you* dating at the moment, Frankie? What happened to that hot-shot surgeon you brought to the Christmas do last year?'

'Long gone.' Frankie pasted a smile on her face. 'Turned out he preferred the girlfriend he had before me so he went back to her. Actually, I don't think he ever broke up with her. He was just, you know, thinking that the grass might be greener on the other side of the fence.'

Mozzie grunted. 'We'll put him on the bastard list too, then.' His gaze shifted from

Frankie to Nico and then back again and he wasn't doing a very good job of hiding a smile or looking like he was having a 'light bulb' moment.

'Oh, come on, Mozzie.' Frankie's tone was sharper than she had intended but she was wincing internally. This was hitting a little too close to home. 'You know that's not going to happen. I'm happily single right now.'

'So am I.' Nico sounded alarmed.

'And surely you haven't forgotten the pact we all made about not dating colleagues?' Frankie was not about to embarrass Nico—or herself—any further. 'You weren't even on the same watch as that paramedic you were dating when I first arrived here and you still threatened to resign and go and work as a crop duster in the outback when it all turned to custard.'

Mozzie grimaced at the bad memory. 'Fair call,' he muttered. 'Right... I'm going outside. My bubble needs washing.'

'And I need to call Jen.' Frankie followed him. She might as well get a bit of fresh air while she made her call and, hopefully, any awkwardness that Mozzie had sparked by the implied suggestion that she and Nico dated each other would be completely forgotten by the time she was finished.

Her call was answered almost immediately.

'Jen?'

'Hey…'

There was something in Jenny's tone that made Frankie pause. 'You busy?'

'Sort of…'

'You sound half asleep. You're not at work?'

'Um…no… Is this urgent?' Jen asked. 'Can I call you back?'

Okay. Frankie had a good idea of what was going on with her friend right now. 'You're with someone,' she said. 'Aren't you?'

'*Frankie…*' The tone was a warning.

'Hey… I'm going.' Frankie was grinning. 'But you have to ring and tell me everything. I wanted to talk dog but it can wait.' She shook her head. 'Eight o'clock in the morning, huh?'

Her grin was subsiding into a smile but it felt like it was only her face involved now. Inside, she had to admit she was feeling a bit…left out?

Envious?

Lonely, even?

'There's no urgency,' she told Jenny. 'I just had a moment and thought I'd check in. Now I'm very glad I did. You go, girl—right back to what you were doing.'

Frankie swiped her screen to end the call. She didn't move from where she was standing, however. She watched Mozzie hosing the bubble-shaped windows on the front of their helicopter to get the dust off and then using a soapy cloth to give them a thorough wash.

She still felt out of sorts. Who was Jenny with? That guy called Rob she had mentioned the night that they'd rescued Bruce? But that was only a couple of weeks ago. Frankie was about to decide it was a bit quick to be jumping into bed with someone, but she had no right to judge her friend, did she? If she'd been offered the chance to get that close to Nico, would she have turned it down?

She couldn't push the thought away quite fast enough to avoid answering her own question. Thank goodness Nico hadn't been remotely interested because Frankie knew perfectly well that an offer like that would have been irresistible.

It was getting easier to keep his distance from Frankie.

After that awkward suggestion from Mozzie that he and Frankie might be interested in each other as more than colleagues, his crew pilot was now finding it fun to try and set him up on blind dates with every single woman associated with South Sydney Air Rescue. And anyone else he knew. Like someone called Donna who worked in the Emergency Response Centre.

'She's cute. In her mid-forties but looks after herself. How old are you, Nico?'

'Thirty-eight.'

'Nothing wrong with dating an older woman. Shall I set it up?'

'*No.*' This wasn't funny any longer. 'Stop, Mozzie. I can find my own woman. If I wanted one at the moment, which I *don't.* I'm too busy. With my job and my new house and looking after my dog.'

My dog. Because it looked as though no one was coming forward to claim Bruce, and Nico was more than happy about that. He was also very happy in the place he'd found to live with Bruce. He could carry his paddleboard down to the sea, through the reserve to where he'd found a place where the cliff was low enough to be easy to navigate a few steps and there was a tiny beach where Bruce could sit in a shady spot. The exercise was helping his leg now and Nico was hoping that Bruce might be persuaded to go swimming one day soon, which might be even better than a shower with the hose at work to keep him clean.

The best time to head for the sea was after work, with summer evenings still staying light enough to get home even well after a sunset at about seven-thirty p.m. Today was the best yet, with a sunset not far away that was promising to light up the sky in glowing shades of red as Nico paddled back towards what he was coming to think of as *his* beach.

Seeing someone climbing down the few steps to the shore was a bit of a shock, to be honest. And, even more surprising, was that Bruce didn't seem bothered. Surely he wasn't actually wagging his tail?

A strong push with his paddle and his board shot forward. It was someone wearing tiny shorts that made her legs look impossibly long and a sports top that doubled as a bra, leaving her midriff bare, and she had running shoes on her feet. Nico didn't need to see the long, dark braid swinging as she bent down to pat Bruce to know who this was.

'Frankie…'

She looked up at his call, straightened and watched as he came back to shore, dropping to kneel on his board and then put one foot down as he felt the sand beneath it.

'I saw Bruce when I was running on the track up there. I thought he might have wandered off by himself and got lost.' She had her hands in the air, as if she needed to emphasise what she was saying. 'I should have known he wouldn't have let you out of his sight.'

Nico was standing beside his board now. 'Perfect timing,' he said.

'Why?'

'Didn't you say you'd always wanted to try a SUP? Now's your chance. There's just enough daylight left.'

'But I'm not wearing my togs. I might fall in and get soaked.'

Oh…there was a thought. But Nico tried to push it aside.

'I'm not wet. See?' His shorts and tee shirt were, indeed, bone-dry. 'You might be a natural and not fall off. But, if you do, it's not far to run home, is it? And it's been such a hot day…'

Frankie looked at him. She looked at the paddle and the board he was holding and then she looked past him to the boats floating on the calm water. The horizon was a glow of pink that was reflecting on the water and Nico knew that she was tempted.

He gave her his most encouraging smile. 'You'll love it,' he said. 'I promise...'

Frankie shrugged. 'Why not? Just a quick go before it gets dark.' She was tugging off her shoes. 'You're right, it's not that far to get home if I get wet.'

Within seconds she was standing in the water beside him. Close enough to feel the warmth of her skin.

'See this, in the middle of the board? It's the carry handle. When you get on, you need to kneel on either side of the handle so that your weight is evenly over the centre line.'

The board wobbled ominously as Frankie climbed on and she gave a surprised squeak. 'I'm going to fall in...'

'No. I've got you.' Nico was steadying the board. He handed the paddle to Frankie. 'Try paddling on your knees to start with.'

Frankie wobbled but then managed a stroke and then another. 'I can do it,' she said delightedly. 'Can I stand up now?'

Nico was standing in water deep enough to be soaking the bottom of his shorts but he wasn't close enough to help Frankie if she fell in.

'You can swim, can't you?'

'I'm not going to fall in. I've got this.' Frankie's grin was wide. 'Just tell me how to do it.'

'Okay.' Nico's hand gesture was one of surrender. 'Put the paddle in front of you across the board and put your hands on it. Put your feet where your knees were and then stand up.'

Frankie wobbled alarmingly this time but managed to stay upright.

'Put your paddle in the water. No…don't look down. You need to look at the horizon— something stable. Start paddling…'

But Frankie was still looking down and she lost her balance and fell into the water with a splash that was big enough to make Bruce bark.

Oh, no… Nico had made a promise that he might have just broken. Frankie might be really annoyed by this unscheduled dunking in cool seawater.

But she was laughing as she surfaced. Nico was wading in a little further to catch the end of the board so he ended up right beside Frankie as she shook the water from her eyes.

'Oops,' she said.

Nico didn't say anything. The light was changing fast around them, as if a dimmer switch had been turned, and he was looking at Frankie's face, with the glow of sunset colours behind it which softened her features and made her smile even more striking. And those eyes...

Dio mio, but she had to be the most beautiful woman Nico had ever seen.

'I'd better get out,' Frankie said. She took a step towards the shore but must have caught her foot on a rock because she stumbled in the waist-deep water and would have fallen in again if Nico hadn't put his hand out for her to catch.

And there they were...standing in the sea with the sun setting around them and...they were touching each other. Frankie was only holding his hand but he could feel the heat from her skin touching his reaching every cell in his body.

Nico felt as if he had rocks beneath *his* feet now. That he was about to fall even though he knew perfectly well he wasn't moving a muscle. He couldn't move. He couldn't look away from Frankie's eyes. And she wasn't moving either.

The paddleboard was drifting towards the shore with the tiny ripple of movement on the surface of the water, but it could have been drifting out to sea right now and Nico wouldn't have even noticed.

Because he was moving now.

Or Frankie was.

It didn't matter who had initiated this because it felt completely inevitable. This had always been going to happen.

This kiss…that felt like it had the power to turn his world inside out and upside down from the instant Nico's lips touched Frankie's.

CHAPTER SIX

OH, DEAR LORD...

Frankie put her foot down to steady her bike as she parked it, turned the engine off and pushed her kickstand into place. As she moved to swing her leg over the seat, cowboy style, to dismount, she could see it in her rear-view mirror.

The red and white Kombi van.

Was Nico still inside his vehicle, which would mean their paths would cross in a matter of seconds? Was he taking Bruce for a walk on the grass to make sure he'd be okay inside for a few hours if necessary or was he already in the building? Having a coffee with Mozzie and Ricky, perhaps, and saying, yeah...it hadn't been a bad night at all, thanks.

Frankie could feel herself cringing.

It was going to be impossible to make eye contact with Nico this morning, wasn't it?

Not because anything horribly awkward or embarrassing had happened.

Oh, no…

Quite the opposite.

Even that kiss had been like no other Frankie had ever experienced. *Ever*…

That first touch had been simply that. No more than a touch. Soft. Brief. Over before it really happened and there'd been that moment of…shock, almost, because it *had* happened. And then, like the afternote of tasting an amazing wine, Frankie had realised that this was different. She was ready for the next brief touch of their lips. And she couldn't wait for the one after that. She'd welcomed the way Nico cradled her head and angled it so that he could explore her mouth with his tongue and Frankie lost all concept of time at that point. She had forgotten she was standing waist-deep in chilly seawater because the heat that this kiss was generating made it irrelevant.

Until she'd shivered. And Nico said it was time to get out.

He said it was not only cold but it was almost dark and he didn't want her to get hypothermia, so she'd better come and dry out at his place before she went home, but they both knew that wasn't the reason she would be going home with him. The sexual tension in the air all around them was so huge, it felt solid. Hard to breathe, even. Had Nico spent that whole, short walk back to his house trying to talk himself out of it? Finding all the reasons, like Frankie was trying so hard to do, why it would be a very bad idea?

Had he worried, like Frankie had, about how awkward it might be arriving at work this morning? She closed her eyes as she eased her helmet off, opening one of the large hard shell panniers on the back of her bike to store it. And then she unfastened the button on her protective overtrousers and pushed them down to take them off.

As she did so, another kaleidoscope of memories cascaded through her head. And her body…

Peeling off those wet shorts.

Loosening her braid to squeeze water out of it with the towel Nico provided.

Lifting her arms so that Nico could peel off the sports top that was still soaked enough to make the skin on her breasts feel icy cold. Or was it just the contrast of the heat of Nico's mouth and tongue that made her skin erupt in goose pimples and her nipples as hard as stone?

Frankie locked her pannier. She took a

slow, deep breath, trying to find the courage to turn and walk into her place of work.

She could do this.

She had no choice.

It wasn't as if it was a 'thing'. They both knew that. There had been a moment, when they arrived at Nico's front door, when either of them could have stopped it happening.

'*Do you want to come in?*' he'd asked softly.

She'd tried, and failed, to take a breath. '*I shouldn't.*'

'You don't have to.'

'*But I want to.*' The admission was torn out of her.

'Me too.'

'*It might make things weird at work.*'

'*It won't. Not if we don't let it.*'

Frankie knew that Nico was watching the way she was biting her bottom lip. She was lost the moment she saw the tip of his tongue touching his own lip, but she had to make sure they understood each other.

'*This can't become...you know...a "thing".*'

'*I don't do "things".*' Nico's smile was wicked. '*This is just for tonight.*'

'*Just this once...?*'

'*Just this once.*'

They had done nothing to be ashamed of.

She and Nico were both single, responsible adults and it had been totally consensual sex.

Except…

Oh, help… Frankie swallowed hard. Except she'd done things she'd never dreamed of doing before. It had been the wildest, *sexiest* sex she'd ever had. She was going to blush the moment she saw Nico, wasn't she? Everybody would guess what had happened last night and they'd both get teased mercilessly. It wouldn't matter that she and Nico had talked about this in the aftermath of that passionate encounter and they'd been firmly in agreement.

'We can't tell anybody.'

Nico had driven Frankie home but stopped far enough away from her house that his van wouldn't have been seen.

'No. Mozzie would claim it was all his idea that we started dating.'

'We're not dating.'

'No…it was just sex…'

'Really? "Just" sex?' Nico's raised eyebrow was teasing.

'No…it was the best sex ever.'

'Yeah… I thought so too. And maybe it's a good thing we broke the rules. We can stop wondering what it would be like now.'

Maybe Nico could stop wondering. Frankie

thought it might be even more distracting now that she knew how good it was. There was still no sign of Nico so she walked inside.

'Morning, Frankie.' Colin smiled at her but didn't stop as he headed for his office carrying a stack of paperwork from the direction of the printer.

Mozzie was beside the stove in the kitchen area. 'You're just in time,' he told her. 'Want a bacon butty? Not you,' he added, looking down to where Bruce was lying right beside his foot. Bruce thumped his tail on the floor and Mozzie shook his head. 'So he wants to be my friend now,' he said sadly. 'Cupboard love, that's all it is.'

Frankie remembered the accusing look Bruce had given her when he'd been shut out of the bedroom last night. It was just as well dogs couldn't talk, wasn't it?

Nico and Ricky were both sitting at the table, eating the sandwiches Mozzie was creating. Nico had his mouth too full to speak but he caught Frankie's gaze for a heartbeat and she could actually feel her level of stress dropping rapidly.

We've got this, his look told her in less than a second. *It's not a problem.*

'They smell so good,' Frankie said to

Mozzie. 'I'd love one if you've got enough for an extra.'

'Always enough for you.' Mozzie had a wad of crispy curls of bacon in the tongs he was holding. 'Grab a piece of bread.'

Colin poked his head out of his office as she took her first, delicious bite of the unexpected breakfast.

'If you get any downtime today,' he said, 'the storeroom needs a bit of a tidy and a stock count for the disposables. I've got to get an order in tomorrow.'

'Sure.' Ricky nodded. 'Be good for Nico to get another look at everything we keep in there.'

Nico nodded, swallowing the last bite of his sandwich. 'I'm getting used to the system here. I really like the way you organise things with colour codes, like the main medical kits and the trauma and paediatric bags. It's so much easier to find and grab when we need to move fast.'

'We know that everything on board is intact because one of my jobs is to make sure it's checked and replaced after every call whenever possible,' Ricky said. 'What we don't want is to find we're low on anything in the storeroom, like airway or IV kit supplies.'

Frankie was just listening, enjoying her

sandwich. Enjoying even more this feeling of normality. She should have known she could trust Nico. She'd certainly trusted him last night…

She had to keep her eyes fixed on her sandwich at that point, pretending to poke a fragment of bacon that was threatening to escape back inside the bread. Because she didn't dare look up and catch Nico's gaze. Not when another round of flashbacks was occupying her brain. So fast they were a blur and yet every instant was recorded in all its glory and every sense, dominated by touch. And taste.

And that feeling of sheer freedom. No inhibition. *Passion*…

There was no way Frankie could take another bite. Not while she could see herself on top of Nico. On *top*…straddling him—her loose hair puddling on his chest as she leaned down to try and kiss him without breaking their rhythm. When she could feel that iron strength in his hands and arms as he flipped her over to reverse their positions and she lifted her legs to wrap them around his waist and let him fill a space she'd never known existed…

'Something wrong with that butty?' Mozzie's

tone was surprised. 'Not like you not to devour your food, Frankie.'

'It's so good, I just wanted to make it last a bit longer.' Frankie's gaze grazed Nico's on its way to catch Mozzie's and reassure him about his cooking abilities.

Just the lightest touch of eye contact but she knew that *he* knew what she was thinking about. That he'd caught the subtext in her comment.

That the sex had been so good, maybe that could last a bit longer as well? That 'just this once' could be repeated?

If so, they would have to keep it secret, which could be tricky now that they knew too much about each other. Nico knew about that unique birthmark Frankie had on her butt cheek that was shaped remarkably like a frog. Frankie knew that Nico had been a daredevil in his teenage years and collected a few scars in hidden places from stupid exploits he probably wouldn't want his colleagues to know about. He hadn't wanted to tell even Frankie about them. Maybe she'd been right about him having a terrifying encounter with someone wielding a knife and she could understand that he wouldn't want to talk about it. Her curiosity had grown, however, as she'd slowly traced the damaged skin on one of his shoulders with her fingertips and perhaps Nico had realised that she wanted to ask questions that he really didn't want to answer. It had certainly been what had finally broken the mood last night and sent Frankie back home, in still damp clothes, for an extremely late dinner.

More importantly, if anything else happened between them, it would have to be a secret so that it wouldn't impinge in any way on their professional relationship. Nico had been confident that they could prevent it getting weird and, so far, that seemed to be working but could the boundary between work and play be solid enough if it happened again?

Did Frankie really *want* it to happen again?

It might have been the best sex ever, but that was all it was.

Nico was happily single and wanted to stay that way for ever.

Frankie was also single, but only until she met the right man to fall in love with. The one who would want to be with her for ever and help create the family that was what Frankie wanted so much in her life. But maybe this had been meant to happen—just for a while.

Because Frankie was beginning to realise it might be a good idea to loosen rules that might have been holding her back without her even knowing.

She could learn to let go of those restrictions she had placed on the type of man she wanted to be with, and that had to be a good thing.

And she was already learning things about herself that were quite the revelation. Sex would never be the same and...that was a good thing too, as long as she didn't allow herself to fall in love with Nico, because that would change *too* much. It might make it impossible to settle for less than the things that were perfect about him and that might mean she would lose the opportunity to find a partner who was ready to settle down and create the family she dreamed of having. In the worst-case scenario, she could fall so deeply in love that she was ready to give up the dream of marriage and children, only to regret it later, when it was too late to do anything about it. And that might ruin her life.

No. That wasn't going to happen. Last night had been empowering in more ways than sexually. Frankie was capable of more than she'd ever given herself credit for, wasn't she?

This time, she deliberately let her gaze catch Nico's.

You're right, she communicated silently. *We have got this*.

She knew the answer to that other question too.

Yeah…she really wanted it to happen again. At least once more, anyway…

Nico let his breath out without having realised he'd been holding it.

He'd wondered how it would be with Frankie this morning but he could finally relax, knowing that it wasn't going to be a big deal.

What had happened had happened and the sex had been astonishingly good, but he wasn't about to start dating Frankie. He wasn't about to start 'dating' anyone. Not if it meant that a relationship might be seen as more than friendship and that expectations would be created. That was never going to happen.

The kind of trust that required had been broken irreparably.

He had got the distinct feeling, thanks to that look she'd given him after saying that her sandwich was so good she wanted it to last longer, that Frankie might be up for indulging in another one-off encounter some time but if avoiding sparking any kind of expectation meant that would never happen, so be it.

But… *Dio mio*…how good had that sex been?

He knew that kind of passion was playing with fire, but he also knew how badly burnt you could get if you let it get out of control, in more ways than the obvious. And he knew himself well enough to know he was more than capable of keeping himself safe.

He wasn't concerned about any awkwardness between himself and Frankie after that reassuring glance she'd just given him. The fact that they could communicate so well with no more than a glance was a worry, however. Would it be added to the physical attraction of this woman, that had not exactly been dampened by last night's adventure, and interfere with his focus on his job? Even as the thought formed, a call came in for a Priority One response, meaning there was an immediate threat to life.

Within seconds, the whole team was standing in front of an aerial map that covered an entire wall of this huge room, and Nico knew that he had nothing to worry about. The mission they were about to embark on was the only thing filling his mind.

'Somewhere around here.' Colin pointed

to a green patch on the edge of one of the national parks south of Sydney. 'Someone saw him come down. No one's found exactly where it's landed yet, but local emergency response is heading in that direction.'

'That's around Wallaby Flats,' Mozzie said. 'I know it. You could find a decent area to land if you were in trouble and there are plenty of forestry tracks that will cater for large vehicles like a fire truck.'

'And it was a microlight, not a hang-glider?'

'Yep.' Colin's face was grim. 'It would be travelling faster.'

'And landing a lot harder,' Frankie added. 'Let's go…'

The air rescue crew received an update en route to the scene. The location had been found and an ambulance and fire truck had arrived. The pilot of the microlight plane was conscious but trapped in the wreckage of the aircraft and the only injuries found on a primary survey were a compound fracture of his left tibia and a painful, bruised neck after being caught by one of the wires supporting the wing structure that had snapped on impact.

Frankie caught Nico's gaze at that information and they didn't need to say anything aloud. They both knew that a neck injury was a huge red flag. If the injury was associated with swelling and bleeding, they could find themselves dealing with an airway emergency and that was something that was far more likely to be fatal than a broken leg. The A for airway was the first part of the ABC of first response for a very good reason.

They didn't play a secret game of rock, paper, scissors to see who was going to take the lead on this case. Frankie was ahead of Nico as they ducked beneath the helicopter's rotors as soon as they touched down and the first to reach the mangled metal with the only recognisable part of the plane being its nose and front wheel pointing up from the ground.

'We got him free about five minutes ago,' a fire officer told Frankie.

'We got an IV line in while he was still trapped.' The land crew paramedic looked up from where he and his partner were splinting the broken bone in his lower leg. 'He's had five milligrams of morphine.'

'Hey…' Frankie crouched beside the young man. 'I'm Frankie and I've got Nico and Ricky with me. What's your name?'

'Levi.'

'Great name…' Frankie smiled but she was

watching him carefully. His respiration rate was high and his voice sounded very hoarse. 'Are you having any trouble breathing at the moment, Levi?'

'Yeah…my neck hurts…' He coughed, groaned and then wiped his mouth, leaving a streak of blood on the sleeve of the flight suit he was wearing.

Frankie unhooked the stethoscope around her neck. 'I'm going to listen to your breathing, Levi.' She looked up at Nico. 'Can you get some monitor leads on, please? I'd like a full set of current vitals as well. An SpO2 ASAP would be great.'

Levi became increasingly anxious as they worked on him to attach monitor electrodes and get an ECG trace showing on the monitor screen.

'I can't breathe,' he told them. 'It really hurts.'

Frankie examined his neck but even a gentle palpation was enough to make him groan in agony. She could feel the slight crunching of crepitus over his laryngeal structures, which suggested damage—possibly a fracture—to his larynx. This was certainly not a patient they wanted to be intubating in the air if he went into a respiratory arrest because, with the neck trauma, it could be a

very difficult airway to secure. If an endotracheal intubation and using a supraglottic
device failed, they would have to try a surgical airway.

'How far are we from the nearest hospital
by road?' she asked.

'Thirty minutes.'

It had taken them ten minutes to get here
by air and it was only a minute or two further than the base to get to the helipad on the
roof of St Mary's.

Levi's rate of breathing was increasing
and, more worryingly, the level of oxygen
in his blood was dropping to a dangerous
level of less than ninety percent even with a
high flow of oxygen going through his mask.
He looked pale and unwell.

Frankie moved to crouch beside her opened
kit. Nico was opening the kit he'd carried
from the helicopter and he was clearly one
step ahead of her in anticipating what they
might need at any minute. He had an airway
set, including a video laryngoscope, which
could help get a tube past anatomical changes
due to trauma, endotracheal tubes, bougie
wires, laryngeal mask airways and a pouch
containing all the drugs they would need to
sedate and paralyse a patient for a rapid se-
quence intubation.

Frankie spoke so that only Nico could hear her. 'An attempt to intubate carries a risk,' she said. 'If there's trauma that prevents passing the tube, even one attempt, let alone more, could exacerbate the damage and close the airway completely so a backup of an LMA won't be viable.'

'And trauma could make a cricothyrotomy impossible,' Nico added quietly. 'What do you want to do, Frankie? Transport him by road?'

'Frankie?' Ricky was closest to their patient at the moment. He sounded calm but she could hear the warning in his tone. Levi's condition was deteriorating.

It was Nico who turned first and, seamlessly, Frankie moved to assist him rather than lead as they dealt with Levi's imminent respiratory arrest. She drew up drugs and ticked off the RSI checklist as Nico administered the anaesthetic and then prepared to get a tube in to secure the airway as quickly as possible.

'I'll use a smaller tracheal tube, thanks,' he told Frankie. 'Six-millimetre. And no cricoid pressure.'

Frankie could see the intense focus on Nico's face as he crouched over Levi's head and peered at the screen on the video laryngoscope as he inserted the blade.

'It's a mess,' he said. 'I'll have one go, as gently as I can. Is the surgical airway kit good to go?'

'Yes.' Frankie had it open beside her and when Nico sat back on his heels and picked up the bag valve mask to ventilate manually and reoxygenate when his attempt had failed, his glance and nod towards her made her take the lead again to perform the procedure that could well be the last chance for them to get Levi to hospital alive. The clock was ticking and it needed to be done as quickly as possible. Within a minute, preferably.

She tipped disinfectant over his neck after Nico had positioned him with his neck extended and padding to arch his shoulders backwards. She held the larynx as carefully as she could with one hand while she made a midline incision into the skin, subcutaneous tissue and cricothyroid membrane, sending up a silent plea that there wouldn't be any major damage at a lower level in the trachea.

Using a bougie wire, she guided an endotracheal tube in place and then inflated the cuff and secured it. Nico was ready to attach and squeeze the bag valve mask to watch for inflation of the lungs on both sides, which would indicate a successful placement. Listening with a stethoscope was next on the checklist and then they could hook the tube up to their portable ventilator and, if they were happy with how stable Levi was and with the help of all the expert personnel still on scene, they could take off within a matter of minutes and get him to where he needed to be—in a well-equipped emergency department with an operating theatre on standby.

It wasn't until much later, when Frankie and Nico had their kits open in the back of the helicopter and they were replacing every item and drug that had been used, that she realised she hadn't given a single thought to Nico as anything but a professional colleague.

The best she'd ever had.

Roles, especially in procedures like airway management, were usually assigned and kept to in order to avoid confusion or wasted time on scene, but working with Nico was almost like working with another version of herself and they could communicate so easily that it felt natural to cross boundaries and simply work together to do what was needed.

They were a perfect match.

And it was only then that the first *unprofessional thought Frankie had had since that shared breakfast entered her mind.

That perhaps they were a perfect match in bed as well as working together?

She waited for that thought to lead to an uncontrolled montage of flashbacks to their night together that could have left her totally distracted, but it didn't happen. Quite the opposite, in fact, and it was a relief that she could just move them to one side—to be revisited later, but only if she chose to do that.

'We need more size six endotracheal tubes for both the airway and the surgical kits,' she told Nico.

'Onto it.' Nico had the drug kit open. 'How good was it to hear that Levi's stable in ICU now? Do you think we could go and see him the next time we're at St Mary's?'

'I think we should.' Frankie nodded. 'It was good to know he's made it through. Looked a bit dodgy there for a while, didn't it?'

She was smiling as she turned back to their task. They had dealt with a very challenging case today and had, undoubtedly, saved a life.

Which meant they *did* also have this situation between them under control. They weren't about to start 'dating', but their unexpected attraction to each other that had led to sex hadn't interfered at all with their ability to work together.

Which meant there was no reason not to allow it to happen again, was there?

If Nico wanted it to happen again, of course.

As much as she did…

CHAPTER SEVEN

THERE WASN'T GOING to be any kind of Indian summer on the east coast of Australia this year.

As autumn gained momentum over the next few days, it seemed like it was already raining far more than usual. Surface flooding was enough to be intermittently cutting access on some inland roads, which meant air rescue helicopters were needed at times to transfer patients who would normally have travelled to hospital by ambulance or their own vehicles.

Red Watch was being kept busy with extra calls using up any downtime between emergencies. Rain wasn't enough to stop the SSAR helicopters flying, unless it was a storm with the potential for hail or lightning which could cause millions of dollars' worth of damage on top of making a flight challenging enough to be dangerous. Mozzie was keeping a very close eye on all the aviation weather maps and detailed forecasts and information coming in from other pilots of both fixed wing planes and helicopters.

'This isn't going away any time soon,' he grumbled during their lunch break. 'The long-term forecast for the rest of March is awful. We'd better start digging our gumboots out. I'm going to go and put new windscreen wipers on the chopper. I can sense an imminent summons for an air taxi to get over the puddles.'

'You might be able to paddleboard to work soon,' Frankie told Nico as both Mozzie and Ricky wandered off. 'You could teach Bruce to sit on the end of the board.'

'Funny you should say that. He swam out to meet me when I was coming back to shore last night. He did his best to get on the board, but ended up tipping me into the water.'

Frankie laughed but made the mistake of holding Nico's gaze a heartbeat too long and she knew they were both remembering her falling off the board and what had happened afterwards.

Only two days ago.

But it felt like for ever.

Who was going to make the first move? Was Frankie brave enough to test the water, so to speak, and see what Nico's response might be?

Yeah... That curl of desire deep in her belly was quite enough of an encouraging push.

'Let me know next time you're going down to that beach. I wouldn't mind having another go myself.' Frankie could feel her cheeks getting warm. 'At paddleboarding,' she added hurriedly.

Nico's eyes had a glint that suggested he was silently laughing at her. 'I'll probably go tonight because Bruce loves his walk, but it's still going to be raining.'

Frankie shrugged. 'It's not that cold. And I'd probably fall in again and get wet anyway.'

'Fair call.' Nico lowered his voice even though they were currently alone in the staff area. 'I might know a good way to warm up too.' One of Nico's eyebrows moved just enough for Frankie to know that he knew exactly what was on Frankie's mind. And that he was happy that she'd made the first move. It wasn't going to stop him teasing her, however. 'A hot shower,' he said. 'Or something hot to eat. I still owe you dinner, don't I?'

'But can you actually cook?' It was Frankie's turn to raise her eyebrows. 'I can't remember any Italian men in my neighbourhood even setting foot in a kitchen. They weren't likely to be able to cook anything other than a prawn or a steak on a barbecue.'

Nico made a very Italian movement with his hand to dismiss the insult. 'My *mamma* and my sisters were determined to teach me. My best dishes are lasagne, chicken parmigiana, calzone, risotto and gnocchi.'

'Do you make your own gnocchi?' Frankie was remembering asking Nico to dinner at her house that night. When they were talking about pasta *alla gricia*.

'*Certamente.*' Nico looked offended again by the suggestion that he might buy the gnocchi ready-made.

'And the sauce?'

'Butter and sage. *Cos'altro*?'

'What else, indeed? Frankie used the tip of her tongue to moisten her bottom lip. 'You're making me feel hungry and I've only just eaten my lunch.'

The glint in Nico's eyes was positively wicked now. 'So I can I tempt you?'

So she wasn't the only one remembering that night. The reference to temptation was definitely on another level now, however.

Because they both knew where that temptation would leave them. And how satisfying it could be.

But... Frankie found herself swallowing hard. 'I like working with you,' she said quietly. 'I really don't want that to get weird.'

'We're talking about dinner,' Nico said calmly. 'About being friends? We both know that's all it is, don't we?'

The boundaries were right there. Frankie could touch them and it felt...safe...

'Dinner,' she echoed, nodding. 'And friends... Okay...'

And if that was all it turned out to be, that really was okay. If it turned out that the sex was so good they both wanted to go there again, that would be okay too. More than okay.

Frankie turned away before Nico could see her smile, but she knew he could hear her murmur.

'Maybe just this once.'

There was a break in the weather that evening but the plan for Frankie to have another paddleboarding lesson didn't quite happen.

Nico was putting potatoes in the oven to bake when she arrived at the beach house.

'We've got at least an hour before they're cooked enough for me to scoop them out to make the gnocchi,' he told her. 'Plenty of time before it gets dark.'

'Mmm...' Frankie had picked up a leafy bunch from the bench beside him and held it to her nose. 'Fresh sage...' But the mention of daylight ending had reminded her of why she had wanted to be here so much, and it had very little to do with eating dinner.

It seemed that Nico had caught her thought. He took the bunch of sage from her hand and put it to one side. As she turned towards him he lifted his hand and touched her cheek with his fingertips, slowly tracing the shape of her face until he could drag his thumb across her bottom lip. Whatever heat the oven beside her was generating in order to bake those potatoes was insignificant to the fire Nico had just ignited and he knew it.

Or maybe he was feeling it just as much as she was. Frankie closed her eyes as she saw him begin to tilt his head, his gaze fixed on her mouth, but she tipped her head back a little to prolong this delicious anticipation and then felt his lips against her neck. On that point where her pulse would be felt so easily so Nico would know exactly the effect he was having on her body. When he finally claimed her mouth with his own, Frankie wrapped her arms around his neck and Nico lifted her against him. She wrapped her legs around his body and he carried her like that, into his bedroom, kicking the door shut behind him to ban Bruce from being a witness to what was about to happen in that room.

They had at least an hour, but it seemed to be over in a blink of time. Oddly, however, it also felt as if time had stopped completely from the moment Nico touched her body so intimately, his lips still covering hers until, eventually, they were lying curled up as closely as possible in his bed, waiting to catch their breath and let their heart rates get back to normal.

It was Nico who untangled himself with a sound of reluctance. 'I need to turn the oven off,' he said. 'Don't move…'

Frankie only moved enough to sit up against the pillows and pull up a sheet to cover herself. Nico came back with a bottle of wine, two glasses and Bruce padding behind him.

'We need to wait for the potatoes to cool down or I'll burn my fingers scooping out the insides,' he said. 'So I thought we may as well be comfortable, seeing as I haven't got any chairs to sit on yet.'

Sitting in bed, sipping an excellent red wine, with Bruce happily asleep on the floor beside them was intimate in a completely different way than their lovemaking had been, but Frankie knew it was something she would also remember for the rest of her life. She leaned her head against Nico's shoulder, letting her breath out in a contented sigh—completely in the moment, without any thought to her past or what the future held—feeling as safe and happy as anyone could dream of being.

'It's been a good day,' she said softly. 'Despite being too much of a flying taxi.'

'The best part is still to come,' Nico said. 'You haven't tried my gnocchi yet.'

Frankie laughed. As if Nico could provide anything better than what he'd just given her. She had something she'd been saving to give him too, and now seemed the perfect time.

'You remember the call we had to Willhua today? When we had to delay the transfer of that woman to Sydney because we got caught in that storm?'

'Of course. You deserted us to go and have coffee with your friend, Jenny.'

'I did. And I was waiting for a break to tell you about it, but we got so busy I kind of forgot and then I thought I'd keep it as a nice surprise.'

'Tell me,' Nico demanded. 'The suspense is killing me.'

'You know Jen's been looking after Bruce's mate, Stumpy?'

'*Sì*...'

'Well, she told me that they haven't found a single relative or friend of Charlie's so nobody's going to claim them. You get to keep Bruce, if you want to.'

Nico was smiling. 'Of course I want to,' he said. 'You're right. Today *is* a very good day.'

She could taste the wine on his lips as he kissed her.

'I'm glad you're happy.'

'Jenny must be happy too. She will keep Stumpy?'

'Yes...'

'You don't sound so happy about that.'

'Oh, I'm delighted that the dogs have found forever homes with people who love them. I'm just a bit worried about Jenny, that's all. I think she's met someone she really likes, but she's running away from him.'

'Why would she do that?'

'Do you know the reason why she resigned from her job with us?'

'Mozzie and Ricky were telling me about it while we were waiting for the storm to pass,' Nico admitted. 'She was in a relationship with the CEO of the SSAR and then found out he was married.'

'Yeah... She was so humiliated, she put in her resignation almost immediately. A bit prematurely, I thought, because he's gone off to work in New York now. But, what the real kicker is, she's found out this new guy she likes—Rob—is also married.'

'No wonder she's running away, then.' Nico sounded disgusted. 'I would as well. No... I wouldn't be stupid enough to get in too deep, too soon and let history repeat itself.' He drained his wine glass. 'I wouldn't get in at all. Once was more than enough.'

Frankie bit her lip, thinking about his reference to the scalded cat who feared even cold water.

'It's not the same,' she said quietly. 'Rob's married, but his wife's on life support. She's been brain dead for years.'

'Oh...' Nico nodded slowly. 'That is different. But...it's only been a couple of weeks, hasn't it? It's too soon for it to mean too much. That's...*cerca di guai*.'

'Asking for trouble,' Frankie echoed. 'Yeah, I guess...'

Wanting to change the subject now, she lifted her head to catch Nico's gaze but her attention was caught by the rippled patch of skin on his shoulder, high enough to be hidden by a short shirt sleeve, that was one of the scars she had noticed before.

'Tell me again,' she said. 'Was this the one from your mountain biking accident or the one from the time the skyrocket exploded?'

Nico snorted. 'I think it was the time the shark bit me.'

'Of course it was.' Frankie was smiling now, her worries about her friend fading, at least for now.

'It's time to get up,' Nico announced, acting on his words by rolling away from Frankie to put his feet on the floor and stand up. Bruce was on his feet too, his big fluffy tail waving approvingly.

Frankie's smile was fading as she watched Nico pull on his board shorts and then a tee shirt that effectively covered the imperfections that marred his smooth olive skin. The shark bite was a highly unlikely explanation. Exploding fireworks were just as unlikely but…that patch on his shoulder did look like the kind of scar a nasty burn could leave behind.

Whatever… Nico might make jokes, but Frankie knew he didn't want to talk about it. It was part of his past. Like his marriage?

She could respect that. The last thing Frankie wanted to do was to push boundaries that could rebound and push her away from Nico. And if he wanted to protect himself, for whatever reason, by making light of past injuries, that was fine too. An air of mystery was just another dollop of sexiness, wasn't it?

By the time Frankie was dressed and had done her best to tidy her tangled mane of hair, Nico had scooped out and mashed the still steaming insides of the baked potatoes and was making dough by adding flour. He certainly knew what he was doing. Frankie leaned on the counter beside him and watched the deft movements of his hands as he brought the dough together and then took parts of it to roll into snakes to cut into small tubular pieces. The really impressive skill was the way he used the tines of a fork to shape the gnocchi ready to drop them into a pan of boiling water.

'They need the ridges,' he explained, when he caught Frankie watching him. 'It makes them hold the sauce better. My sister Rosa taught me that.'

'Good for her,' Frankie said approvingly. 'Maybe the undesirable gender roles I grew up with will start changing if there are more women like your sisters.'

'You love Italian food, but you don't like

Italian men.' Nico's sideways glance was curious.

'I like you,' Frankie said lightly.

'Because I can cook?'

'Yes.' Frankie lifted her hands, her palms facing upwards. 'And it may be that I've been misjudging other Italian men because I've based my opinion on a previous generation and I will take that into account in the future. It has been a long time since I decided I didn't like Italian boys.'

'What did they do to you?'

'They wouldn't let me play football in the street with them and it was all I wanted to do when I was ten years old. They told me to go home because I was only a *girl*.'

Nico laughed. 'I bet they changed their mind about playing with you when you were older.'

'That was even worse.' Frankie's hand gestures were sharper now. 'It was all wolf whistles and honking car horns and shouts of *"Bella*, come out with us…". And eyes everywhere, blatantly undressing me. By the time I was old enough to be allowed out, I had sworn I would never date an Italian boy.'

Nico put the last gnocchi into the boiling water. His hand was still covered in flour when he cupped Frankie's chin and leaned in to place a slow, sexy kiss on her lips. 'It's just as well we're not dating, then, isn't it?' he murmured.

'Just as well.' Frankie still had her eyes closed. She opened them to find Nico smiling at her.

'I will play football with you if you wish,' he offered. He put a large slice of butter into a pan to melt.

Frankie laughed, but his words touched a part of her heart that she hadn't thought about for many, many years. That part that had been so lonely when she was an only child. When she'd wanted so desperately to be allowed to join those football games. There had been girls to hang around with, but little Frankie had had no interest in dolls or make-up or, later, hanging around in shopping malls to look at clothes or jewellery and talk about nothing but boys.

She watched Nico chop the sage leaves to go into the butter.

Mr Perfect.

He wasn't just gorgeous to look at or so good at his job which had been enough for her to rethink her teenage vow and even believe that she could fall in love with Nico Romano. She now knew that he was the most passionate lover any woman could dream of. That he was kind to dogs and small girls and not-so-small girls. And he could cook. Frankie didn't need any more than the smell of the burnt butter and sage and the sight of soft, light gnocchi floating in the boiling water, ready to be served, to know that this dinner was going to be as perfect as everything else about Nico.

Almost everything else, she reminded herself.

Nico was the scalded cat. She could still hear the resolute tone of his voice when he'd said he would never get in too deep, too soon. That he would never get in at all, in fact. He was running just like Jenny was, but had he been doing it so long it had become an automatic part of his life? A part of who he was? Was it a rule he'd made that might need to be revised—like her antipathy to a man simply because of his nationality?

Perhaps Jenny was making the same mistake and allowing an admittedly justified prejudice to blind her to something that might, in fact, be completely different.

And maybe it *was* only two weeks since Jenny had met her man. But it was only two weeks since Frankie had met Nico and, if things were different, she could have been quite sure that she had found exactly what she hadn't known she was actually looking for. Two weeks wasn't too soon for it to mean something significant.

This—what she'd found so unexpectedly, with a man who shared her heritage—could have meant everything.

But Nico *had* been right about something else. Getting in so deep so soon was asking for trouble.

And Frankie had a horrible feeling she *was* in trouble. She hadn't meant it to happen but it was beginning to feel a lot like when she'd fallen off that paddleboard. She'd had no chance of stopping it happening.

So much for boundaries.

So much for brushing off how she felt about Nico as some sort of fantasy she could enjoy and then leave behind. Or believing that she could break the very sensible rule of not dating a colleague because of the potential fallout. Thinking that it might be good for her to learn to let go of the barriers she'd put in place in her own life, even.

Okay…they weren't 'dating'. Not officially, anyway. And maybe Nico was capable of being attracted enough to someone to be able to experience the kind of passionate lovemaking he'd introduced her to and not start falling in love with that person, but Frankie had overestimated her ability to control what was happening to both her body and her heart.

Somewhere, in the blink of time that two weeks represented in a lifetime, she might have already given too much of both her body and her heart to Nico Romano. How could she have believed she could stop herself falling in love with this man? The warning signs had been there right from the first moment she'd met him but, even then, she suspected it would have been too late to save herself.

It was just as well Nico had no idea how she felt about him because he'd made it very clear that it was the last thing he would want.

To her horror, Frankie could feel tears prickling at the back of her eyes. To hide them, she stooped to scratch behind Bruce's ears.

'You're a lucky dog,' she told him. 'And nobody's going to take you away because Nico loves you.'

Oh…this was already harder than she'd thought it would be.

This yearning to be loved by Nico herself, even when she knew it would never happen. It was so strong, it was actually a physical pain.

'And you're going to love this…' Nico was holding out a bowl with a generous serving of his gnocchi and sauce. 'You have a choice,' he told her.

Did she?

Frankie didn't feel like she had a choice at all. If she did, she would have been sensible and not allowed herself to get in too deep, too soon, with Nico. She wouldn't be here now, making things harder for herself by sinking even further into these feelings. She knew perfectly well that, at some point, she was going to have to deal with another broken heart but, when the only choice was whether to do that now or put it off as long as possible so that she could enjoy every moment of being with Nico while it lasted, it was a no-brainer. She wanted this.

No… It felt more like she *needed* it.

Like oxygen. Or light. And food… Inhaling the familiar aroma of the sage was a way back to the present and being able to shut down her line of thought.

'I promise I will find a table and chairs or a couch before you come to have dinner next time,' Nico said as Frankie accepted the bowl. 'For now, we can sit in the van to eat, on the steps of the veranda, although we might get rained on, or we can go back to bed.'

'The veranda,' Frankie decided. 'The van if it starts raining.'

Definitely not the bed. She might end up with those tears actually escaping.

Frankie might not have a choice she was capable of making about whether or not to be with Nico but, if she wanted it to last for even one more 'just this once', she had to make sure he wasn't aware of how she felt. Instinct told her that if he knew, he would run a lot further and faster than Jenny was running away from Rob. So fast, Frankie would lose sight of him instantly.

Not in a physical sense, because they would still have to work together, but she would never see the glimpses of the intimate connection they'd made in those shared, meaningful glances or a secret code running beneath an innocuous comment. They'd probably never play rock, paper, scissors again to decide who would lead the assessment and treatment of a patient. Was it possible that it could be so uncomfortable that one of them would end up requesting a transfer to a different watch, or even move on to a new job?

No. It was within Frankie's power to not let that happen and it wasn't as if she'd never had any practice. Those boys who had refused to let her play football with them had never known how bad it had made her feel. She could remember the way she'd tossed her hair and walked away with a smile on her face.

I don't care... I've got better things to do today, anyway...

And hadn't Nico all but promised there would be a 'next time'—when he had chairs or a couch for them to sit on?

Frankie didn't need to think about anything other than how good it was to be here right now. She certainly didn't need to cry about something that hadn't even happened yet.

Maybe it wouldn't happen for a very long time. Long enough for Nico to realise that he could safely break his own rules, perhaps?

Suddenly, it was easy to smile at Nico. *'Deliziosa,'* she said, having swallowed her first bite of the meal he'd prepared with such care. 'I *do* love this. *Grazie molte...'*

Life couldn't get any better than this, could it?

A few days later, Nico felt like his heart was filling to the point of being in danger of bursting as he looked down to where his dog was sitting, proud and tall, on the front of his paddleboard—like one of those carved wooden figures that used to be on oceangoing ships to give protection to its crew and safeguard their homeward journey.

Bruce was wearing the bright orange canine life jacket Nico had sourced online. The handles on the top had solved the problem of the large dog tipping him off by trying to scramble on board. He'd quickly learned to stand or swim alongside and let Nico lift him out of the water. Because he trusted him. And the love, that was growing every day, went both ways. Bruce had become a whole lot more than simply a pet. He was another living being that was sharing his life. One who could be trusted a hundred percent to be loyal and loving and…and so happy to be with him because he thought Nico was perfect.

Well… Bruce was the perfect dog. How lucky was he that he was a part of Nico's life now and that nobody was going to try and take him away?

Nico had to shake his head to get rid of trickles of water coming from his hair and threatening to get into his eyes. Okay… maybe life could get a bit better with an improvement in the continuing unstable weather patterns, but neither he nor Bruce minded being out in the drizzle this evening, especially with the water so calm he could see their reflection as they moved past the moored boats on the way back to shore. He had old towels at home that he could dry Bruce with and a quick, hot shower would be just as effective for himself.

Or maybe he'd just use an old towel as well and wait until he could share that hot shower later this evening. With Frankie...

She was out shopping right now because it was her turn to cook. Nico put a bit more effort into his paddling until he could feel the muscles in his shoulders burning. He needed a bit more exercise because it seemed like he and Frankie had started competing to see who could create the most delicious Italian food. She was making Caprese pizza tonight. She'd promised homemade dough for a crispy base, soft mozzarella cheese, juicy tomatoes and fresh basil with a balsamic glaze that was one of her *nonna*'s closely guarded secrets.

Nico could actually hear his stomach growl.

Life *was* about to get a whole lot better. Because there would be amazing food. Quite probably even more amazing sex. And because, like Bruce was the perfect dog, Frankie was the perfect friend. She was loud and funny and warm, but she was also highly intelligent and extremely talented and so damned sexy but wasn't making any demands on him for any kind of commitment. They both knew this was never going to last. Nico didn't do deep. And he didn't do long-term. Frankie understood that. She'd known right from the start that he wasn't remotely interested in getting married again so, of course, this was never going to be anything serious.

Even saying 'just this once' had become a private joke but the truth was there, hiding in plain sight. It had to stop, but neither of them seemed to want it to stop quite yet because it was just too good? Maybe it should be worrying Nico that this was going on longer than maybe either of them had foreseen, but it was easy to reassure himself. They had, on more than one occasion, agreed that this was not a 'thing'. That they were not going to let it interfere with them being able to work together. The longer it went on for, the more important their friendship was also becoming.

Was Frankie confident that, when the time came, it would be easy to walk away?

Nico felt something like a chill run down his spine. Because it was getting colder out here on the water? Or were his thoughts veering towards considering something that was out of bounds. That, if things were different, he might have been able to be a man Frankie would choose to keep in her life.

But he wasn't that man. He couldn't be, no matter how much he might want to be, because he would always be haunted by the destruction the slow downward spiral of his marriage had wreaked over far too long a timespan. The echoes of Sofia's endless criticism that had proved how disappointing she'd found him would always be there. He had never been able to do anything right. He hadn't cared enough about her because he'd spent too much time with his family—alone, because Sofia had grown to hate disappearing into the crowd of big gatherings.

Sometimes, he could still feel a frisson of the humiliation in the way she had used affection as a reward and the withholding of it as a punishment and he never knew which side the spinning coin would land on. How many thousands of times had he heard about how unhappy he'd made her and how useless he was as a husband and a lover? That it was *his* fault she lost her temper so often? And how unforgettable had that vicious question been of how he could possibly think that anyone would ever want him to father their children?

Frankie didn't know anything about any of that and he wanted to keep it that way.

He'd found a career he was both passionate about and good at. He'd discovered that he was also far better at sex than Sofia had given him credit for.

And that was enough. He could never risk his heart again. Not when it felt like it had only just been glued back together properly.

Why would he even consider doing that when life felt *this* good just the way it was right now?

Getting home to the rundown beach house with his beloved Kombi van parked outside it at the end of the long drive was something else to be grateful for in this new life of his.

It felt like home.

It would feel even more like home when Frankie arrived with her bags full of fresh ingredients. It might be her turn to cook, but she was coming to his place to make the meal. Because they both knew that the passionate lovemaking they were both so into was not always quiet and they wanted to protect their privacy. Or was it that they both knew that if it became known, the people around them— friends, housemates and colleagues— would make it a 'thing'. That maybe they would all think that he and Frankie were perfect for each other and, somehow, they would find out how wrong they were?

That Frankie would find out the shameful secret of just how appalling his marriage had been? How much of a failure he'd been as a husband?

If they stopped this now, before they got any closer, she'd never need to find out. But Nico didn't want to stop. Not just yet. Not even if it was going to be so much harder when he had no choice.

Because it was the combination of having both Bruce and Frankie in his life that was making it so good. Between them, they were filling the gaps that had been there ever since he'd left his homeland and family behind.

It was no wonder that this little blue house felt like home when they were all here together. The Italian food was a bonus.

And the sex was the icing on that proverbial cake.

Oddio… Nico was starving now. For much more than simply food. He found himself closing his eyes to cope with the shaft of sheer desire that speared his gut when he heard the muted roar of a motorbike coming up his driveway.

CHAPTER EIGHT

RAIN FALLING ON the already sodden ground surrounding Sydney, especially inland and to the south, had nowhere to go so it lay on the surface of farmland and roads and got steadily deeper. River levels were rising and dams getting too full. There was talk of 'one in one hundred years' flooding events and of areas that were predicted to receive six months' worth of their annual rainfall in a matter of only days. Evacuations were happening to prevent people getting cut off and losing all normal services including health care but, even with the best intentions of heeding the warnings, there were some who found they'd left it too late to get out in time.

Like the woman in labour, two weeks earlier than expected, whose husband had begun driving her to her nearest hospital only to find a bridge had just been washed out and she was completely cut off. They went back to their farmhouse and called for help. The young farmer was able to use his dogs and clear a mob of sheep from a paddock high enough to not be covered in water and close enough for a helicopter to land so that Nico and Frankie got only moderately wet by the time they'd carried their equipment through the heavy rain and up the steps to the shelter of the wide veranda of a traditional square Australian farmhouse.

When they saw the woman walking down the hallway to greet them, it seemed like the plan for a quick load and go was on track. The labour suite in the nearest hospital would be the safest place for her to give birth and Mozzie hadn't shut down the helicopter in the expectation of an imminent take-off. Their patient's husband was right behind her, carrying a suitcase and another bag and, further down the hallway, was an older woman who was holding two small children by the hands.

'No, you can't go with Mummy,' Nico heard her say. 'But you can give her a kiss goodbye and we can watch the helicopter take off. Won't that be fun?'

'No...' One of the toddlers was crying. 'We want to go too...'

Nico had just changed his mind about this being a quick pick-up. Because he had just noticed a trail of drips on the polished wooden floorboards of the hallway.

But he was smiling at the woman. 'It's Shannon, isn't it? I'm Nico and this is Frankie. How far apart are your contractions now?'

'About six or seven minutes, I think. Ben's been timing them...'

Shannon's husband checked his watch. 'Last one was four and a half minutes ago. It lasted about sixty seconds. This is faster than it was with the twins.'

'And your waters broke a while ago?' Frankie asked. She was looking at the floor between Shannon's feet and Nico could see the way her face had gone still as she processed what she thought she might be seeing.

'That was why we started driving towards the hospital.' Ben nodded. 'Mum said the river was running high when she came over to look after the twins for us, but we couldn't believe our eyes when we got into the valley and the bridge was just...gone...'

'It was really scary,' Shannon said. 'Thank goodness you guys got here as fast as you did. I've got my bags ready. It's okay if Ben comes with me, isn't it?'

'Of course. But we'd like to check what's happening for you before we head out to the helicopter, if that's okay. Things like your blood pressure and the baby's heart rate.'

'I'd rather get going,' Ben said. 'We don't want to end up having a home birth. Not in this weather. We might be on a hill but we can't afford to be stranded with a newborn baby, not when he's already making his appearance too early.'

'And we need to know what we might be dealing with before we're in the air.' Nico kept his tone calm. 'How long have you been bleeding for, Shannon?'

'What?' Shannon looked down. 'Oh... that's just my waters, isn't it? I must need to change the pad I'm wearing.'

Nico stooped to touch the dark floorboards with his gloved finger. It was bright red when he held it up and both Shannon and Ben looked shocked.

'What's going on?' Ben demanded.

'That's what we need to find out.' Frankie put her hand on Shannon's arm, turning her back towards the interior of the house. 'Have you got somewhere close that you could lie down, Shannon? And some old towels we could cover a bed or couch with?'

Ben was still staring at them, his face pale. Shannon reached for his arm to steady herself as she bent forward. 'It's another one,' she groaned. 'Oh…this one really hurts…'

They couldn't ask Shannon to move until the contraction was over. Nico estimated that it was only five minutes since the last one, it lasted a good ninety seconds and Shannon was still bleeding. He radioed Mozzie.

'You can shut down, mate,' he told him. 'I don't think we're going anywhere just yet. Come inside. We might need an extra set of hands. Could you bring some towels too?'

Ricky had been left behind because this was only supposed to be a patient transfer and they weren't sure how many passengers they might be dealing with. Shannon was trying to stifle a loud cry with the pain of her contraction and the two toddlers were shrieking, Ben almost tripped over one of the bags he'd dropped as he moved to put both his arms around his wife and the older woman looked as frightened as he did. A dog had appeared from nowhere and started barking at the spectacle and this whole scene had suddenly turned into a bit of a circus.

Frankie's housemates had jokingly warned him that she was bossy but he'd never seen her take charge quite like this.

'Okay, that contraction is easing, isn't it, Shannon? Try and slow your breathing a bit

and save some of that energy. Ben? You and
Nico get on either side of Shannon and help
her lie down somewhere.' She turned her
head to look through the nearest door. 'That
couch is fine.' She turned back. 'Nana, take
the little ones into the kitchen for the moment. And the dog too, please. Put the kettle
on and make yourself a cup of tea.'

The instructions were rapid-fire and in
a tone that was not to be argued with. The
children and dog magically disappeared
with their grandmother and the noise level
faded as a door was closed. They managed
to get Shannon near the door of the living
room with the couch, but that was as far as
she could move before another contraction
started. She sank to the floor to get on her
hands and knees and Nico's heart sank even
further.

They needed to find out whether Shannon
was bleeding enough for it to signify an obstetric emergency like a ruptured uterus or
a placental abruption. They had to find out
if the baby was in distress by monitoring its
heart rate. They needed to get IV access to
give fluids if Shannon's blood pressure was
dropping. The tension was escalating to the
point where Nico felt a knot forming in his
gut. Of all the emergencies they could at-

tend, an obstetric one was his greatest fear—because there were two lives at stake here.

Frankie wasn't showing anything like his own concern. She was crouched beside Shannon, with one hand on her wrist to take her pulse and the other rubbing her back. Between reassurance for Shannon, she was gathering as much information from Ben as possible.

'Have there been any problems at all with the pregnancy?

'When did you have the last ultrasound?

'Is it just one baby this time?

'Do you know what position the baby is in?'

The responses were all reassuring but Nico was starting to unpack all the gear that could be potentially vital, including a birthing and neonatal resuscitation kit.

Frankie still sounded completely in control. 'I need to have a look,' she told Shannon. 'I have a feeling your baby's not going to wait until hospital to make his arrival.'

'It's a girl,' Shannon wailed. 'Oh…it's starting again already. I need to push…'

'Hang on for just a sec.' Frankie was getting Shannon's clothing out of the way. 'Pant for me, love. Like you're blowing out candles. You've done this before. You're an expert…' She was panting herself to encourage Shannon as she knelt behind her. 'Okay…' Her voice was still remarkably calm. 'Baby's crowning. I'm going to put a little bit of pressure on her head so she doesn't arrive too quickly. Breathe through this contraction and you can push with the next one.'

A minute or two later, Nico looked up from opening the drug kit to draw up a dose of oxytocin, which would hopefully control the abnormal bleeding already happening and reduce the risk of a postpartum haemorrhage. He could see that the baby's head was presenting with the contraction. He could also see that the umbilical cord was wrapped around her neck, but even that didn't seem to faze Frankie.

'Stop pushing for a sec, Shannon. Pant again…' Frankie slipped her finger under the cord and looped it over the head. 'Okay… good to go. You're doing brilliantly… One more push should do it.'

Frankie's movements were gentle and controlled as she provided downwards traction to deliver the baby's anterior shoulder and then upwards traction to help deliver the posterior shoulder.

And then the baby was born, a small face

already crumpled and arms raised as she took in her first breath to release a warbling cry. Ben had his arms around Shannon to help her turn to meet their daughter and Frankie took a clean towel from Mozzie, who'd just walked in the front door, wrapped the baby and then lifted Shannon's shirt to put the tiny girl on her mother's chest, skin to skin.

'Is that ten units of oxytocin?' Frankie smiled at Nico. 'Good job. We'll wait a couple of minutes before we cut the cord. Can you do the first Apgar score?' She turned back to their patient. 'I'm going to give you an injection of oxytocin into your thigh,' she told Shannon. 'Are you okay with that? It's going to help with the delivery of your placenta, which is important. It might also help you to not lose any more blood, which would be a good thing.'

Shannon nodded. She was in Ben's arms and they were both looking down at their newborn daughter, but the young mother was shivering violently.

'Mozzie? Could you go and find the *nonna* who's in the kitchen and get her to find a duvet or some blankets?' Nico caught Frankie's gaze. 'One minute Apgar score is five.'

The five-minute Apgar score was eight,

which told them that this baby was doing well despite her precipitous birth. Ben was the one who cut the umbilical cord after Frankie had put the clamps on and the placenta arrived without any indication of bleeding that would cause concern. Wrapped in a puffy duvet, Shannon had stopped shivering.

'Shall I tell Nana that she can bring the boys in to meet their little sister?' Frankie was smiling. 'Then we'll get you all sorted for a trip into hospital.'

Ben's mother burst into tears and rushed out when Frankie opened the door, so she was the one left to cope with two small, excited boys. And the dog who was turning in joyous circles and barking enough to make Frankie shake her head. But she was laughing.

She came towards them with one toddler in her arms, perched on her hip, and holding the hand of the other twin. Nico stepped back to stand beside Mozzie as the whole family, including Frankie, clustered around to admire the new arrival.

And something was melting inside Nico's heart.

She looked so completely at home surrounded by adults, young children and a brand-new baby. Frankie was born to be a mother, wasn't she? The heart of a family like this. She was so calm and competent and she had so much love to give. Those were clearly happy tears she was brushing from her eyes as she cuddled the toddlers and let them look at their sister without getting *too* close. And then she took the baby from Shannon's arms so that Ben could help her into clean clothes and a warm puffer jacket as they started the preparations to take them to hospital for a thorough check. Nico and Mozzie were packing up the gear, but he couldn't help another glance over his shoulder to where Frankie had her head bent over the baby she'd delivered, closing her eyes to place a soft kiss on its head.

She'd look just like that when she was holding her own baby, he thought.

As if it was the most miraculous day of her life.

And Nico's heart was breaking.

Because he would feel like that as well, if she was holding *his* baby.

The yearning had never felt this powerful. So strong it felt like his heart was bleeding. A need that was never going to be realised, because he could never take even the first steps towards that dream when he knew what it was like to fall off the edge of the cliff he hadn't seen coming.

He wanted to take that first step in that moment, more than he'd ever wanted anything. He actually straightened, as if he was about to take a physical step towards Frankie at the same time, but then he froze.

He couldn't do it. His heart might have healed but the glue that was holding the pieces together—that ability to trust—wasn't strong enough yet.

Maybe it never would be. And that meant that it was time to stop wasting Frankie's time. She should be with a man who could give her the joy of having her own baby, and she wasn't going to find him if he was hanging around as anything more than a friend.

But how could he do it without hurting Frankie?

Because that was something he wasn't sure he could bring himself to do. Their friendship was too important.

He cared about her too much.

No. He *loved* her that much...

There was something different about their lovemaking that evening.

Or was it that they were both overtired after a long day and some uncomfortable scenarios due to the bad weather? Neither of them had had the energy to cook a meal, but it was nearly eight o'clock by the time they'd completed the paperwork and restocking the kits and were able to head home. It was Frankie who'd offered to pick up some fish and chips while Nico gave Bruce a bit of a walk in what was left of the daylight.

Neither of them had been planning to go to bed together that night. Nico had a big old couch in his living room now and that was where they sat to share their dinner and a small glass of wine. They didn't even bother with plates or cutlery, but ate their meal from the paper opened on the couch between them.

'I'll have to ride home soon. It might be another big day tomorrow.'

Maybe it was the way Nico was looking at her that made Frankie lean close enough to kiss him, and it was then that she first noticed something different. The ignition point for passionate sex was the same but, for some reason, it felt like Nico was holding back from lighting it. The kiss was tender to the point of being almost heartbreaking.

'You okay?' she asked when she pulled away to catch a breath.

'Sure. Why wouldn't I be?'

Frankie shrugged. 'It's been a long day.

A bit dodgy at times too. Don't know about you, but I was really scared about what was about to happen to Shannon.'

Nico nodded. 'I was too. What caused so much bleeding, do you think?'

'Her cervix might have dilated so abruptly that it broke a few blood vessels.' Frankie blew out a breath. 'I've never seen that much bleeding without it being something major. I had visions of her bleeding to death from a ruptured uterus or an abruption before we could get her to hospital.'

'You didn't look at all scared.' Nico's expression was impressed. 'You handled it *magnificamente*.'

'Thanks… You were pretty awesome yourself. I…' Frankie bit back the words she suddenly wanted to say about what she really thought of him. How she felt about him. Instead, she did her best to keep her expression, and her tone, as light as possible.

'I really like working with you, Nico…' She kissed him again, very lightly. 'I really like…*this*…'

He made a sound that could have been weariness. Or surrender? There was a note of distraction in it. Or maybe it was reluctance? Whatever it was, however, it had gone by the time Nico claimed her mouth properly and she could taste the rising level of desire for them both. One of them, and it might well have been Frankie, pushed the fish and chip wrappers off the couch and she saw the blur of Bruce grabbing a leftover piece of fish and heading for the veranda with his prize before he could be stopped.

Not that either of them had any intention of stopping Bruce from disappearing. Or stopping what they were doing as the kissing deepened and hands moved to shift clothing and gain access to skin. To stroke and touch with the certainty of knowing exactly what to do to increase that arousal to a deliciously unbearable peak.

But even then there was something…different enough about the way Nico was touching Frankie for her to be aware of it.

It wasn't different in a bad way. It might have been a lot less wild, but maybe that was being dictated by the limited space for two people on a couch. It was…*softer*, Frankie decided. The kind of sex that two people who knew each other so well could have if they were a bit tired or distracted but they still needed to be this close. Two people who really cared about each other.

Frankie lay in Nico's arms a little while

later, her head—and her heart—filled with the thoughts she couldn't say aloud.

I love you...

I'm in love with you...

I never want this to stop...

The dreamy bridge between being alert and falling asleep was broken abruptly by the sound of an incoming video call from Nico's laptop that was open on the floor at one end of the couch.

'That might be my sister, Rosa.' He rolled away from Frankie and dragged on his shorts. 'I need to answer it. My mother wasn't so well the other day...' He glanced at his watch as he picked up his computer. 'It's nearly eleven p.m. here so that makes it lunchtime at home.'

Thankfully, Frankie wasn't completely undressed but she hastily did up the buttons on her shirt. How awkward would it be if Nico's sister spotted evidence of what they'd just been doing?

But Nico was walking away with the laptop screen—and its camera—facing only himself as he clicked to accept the call and the sudden joyous shouting from too many loud voices changed the atmosphere in this room so much that Bruce, who'd come back inside to check for any more leftover food, instantly headed for the open front door to escape again.

'Nico...' A woman was laughing and then speaking in Italian that was so fast Frankie had trouble keeping up. 'What time is it for you? Did we wake you up? Is it hot there? It's so hot here today...'

'Uncle Nico...' More than one child was shrieking in the background. 'We miss you...'

'I miss you too, *cara*. And you, Paolo, and you, Tommaso. Are you being good boys for your *mamma*?'

'No.' It was the laughing woman again. 'They are monsters, all of them. When are you coming to visit home again to help me tame them?'

'Soon, I hope. How is Mamma?'

'Much better. She's here too. And your other sisters, but we all know I'm your favourite, yes?' There was increased volume in the background shouting. 'Okay, okay. Just wait... Nico, everybody wants to talk to you...'

Nico was leaning on the kitchen bench, his gaze fixed on the screen, but he looked up and nodded as Frankie waved and slipped out to give him time alone with his family. He blew her a kiss but, as Frankie paused to give Bruce a pat before she left, she took another glance back into the house.

Nico was laughing at something he was seeing now, but he almost looked as if he could burst into tears at any moment and Frankie knew she had just learned something new about this man she had fallen in love with.

He adored his family and they adored him.

The joy in the voices of those children as they'd greeted him reminded Frankie of how he'd been with that little girl and her broken doll.

How could he be so adamant that he never wanted a family of his own?

He would be as perfect a father as it was possible to be. A perfect husband and lover. He was already a precious son and brother and uncle.

Frankie kicked her bike into life and rode off into the rain, but it wasn't dampening her spirits one little bit.

Because it felt like there was hope. Given time, perhaps Nico would realise that, for whatever reason, he'd been lying to himself? And that he wanted exactly the same future that Frankie did?

With her...

CHAPTER NINE

EVERYBODY HAD HAD enough of the rain, especially when yet another deep low-pressure weather system headed straight towards New South Wales. After two days of this new front slowly passing through, there were worrying reports on the news of a potential catastrophe that kept Frankie's best friend, Jenny, constantly in her thoughts.

A good part of south Sydney's drinking water supply came from a huge man-made reservoir in hills about fifty kilometres inland from Willhua and the excessive amount of water it now contained was creating so much pressure that people feared the dam would burst and the ensuing flood would affect everything in its path as it roared downhill towards the sea.

Towards Willhua. And Jenny.

In order to prevent the dam bursting, a release system was activated to lower the water level in the reservoir but, because the entire area was already so sodden that lower-lying areas were flooded, the enormous amount of extra water became a flash flood that turned into a situation that was quickly declared an evolving national disaster. Every resource—including local volunteers in the State Emergency Service, the Red Cross, military, fire, police and ambulance units and every helicopter and boat that could be made available—became part of the massive effort to protect people, livestock and properties.

There were heartbreaking scenes of people desperately trying to save their horses by risking swimming them through the floodwaters or trying to muster sheep or cattle to higher ground and there were lines of cars being guided to roads where the water was not yet deep enough to be dangerous, full of families and pets and whatever precious possessions they'd been able to grab before heading for community halls, churches or schools that were deemed safe and were already being run by volunteers who could provide dry clothing, hot food and access to medical care.

South Sydney Air Rescue was in the thick of it, having all available staff members brought in before first light to be briefed on the situation and rostered for shifts that would continue day and night until the disaster was under control. Bruce had been left in Nico's van because there were so many people milling around the base, but arrangements were made for someone to let him out if Nico couldn't get back to base often enough.

Being trained to operate a winch, Ricky got moved to another crew where they were short of a team member so it was just Mozzie, Nico and Frankie on board. They were allocated blocks of time when they would be available to fly depending on the weather, broken up by long breaks between the active spells. The dangers of the environment and the tasks they would be asked to do were high enough without allowing exhaustion and human error to exacerbate them.

The range of medical intervention needed ranged from full-on drama, going to the aid of a farmer who was in danger of bleeding to death from a partial amputation of his leg, having fallen into hidden farm machinery while trying to move stock to higher ground, to nothing more than reassurance and care in helping to relocate the confused and frightened residents of a retirement home that had

water already several inches deep through-
out the buildings.

A search and rescue mission for a car was
needed when a driver had not heeded the
stern warnings from authorities to stay out
of any floodwaters. The vehicle had gone
into what looked like only a big puddle, to
get caught by an unseen current and swept
into a torrent of water beside the road where
the river was carving a new channel through
rural land. It didn't take long for the Red
Watch crew to spot the small hatchback that
was caught in an island of tangled tree trunks
and other debris and they stayed overhead to
help the police and rescue teams locate the
scene and then waited as they worked to get
to the driver. If they couldn't get to the car,
Frankie or Nico could go down on a winch
line. If they could get to the car and the driver
was injured, they could help with medical
care and evacuation to hospital.

Both Frankie and Nico leaned out of the
open door of the helicopter, watching the
people in their high-vis gear and helmets
gathering to attempt the rescue. They had a
cable attached to the courageous police officer who battled the current of the river to get
to the car, anchored by his colleagues. They
watched as he smashed the window of the car

and managed to prise the door open. They could see the elderly man in the driver's seat.

And they could hear the exchange between Mozzie and the SES team leader below.

'You can stand down, mate. He's deceased. Go somewhere you're really needed.'

'Roger that.' Mozzie's tone was grim. The death toll for this disaster had just increased by one.

He'd no sooner radioed the control centre to say they were headed back to base than another call came in.

'Sorry, guys. We know you're due for a break but you're the closest we've got to a job that's been on the books for too long now. East of Coledale. There's a whole family on the roof of their farmhouse. Two adults and a six-year-old child. They're on the top of the veranda because the roof's too steep, but they've just told us the water's up to the guttering and there's no one else that'll be available any time soon by boat *or* air.'

Mozzie turned his head, knowing that Frankie and Nico had heard the exchange. They both gave him a thumbs-up. Maybe they needed the chance to help people who were still alive before heading back to base and being unable to help anyone for the next few hours.

'Send through the coordinates,' Mozzie told the dispatcher. 'We're on our way.'

They flew low, over a sea of murky brown water dotted with the canopies of trees visible like oversized shrubs and just the corrugated iron roofs of houses and outbuildings still above the water level. It didn't take long to spot the group of people huddled together on the very edge of a roof. A woman was clinging to a young child. There was a plastic pet crate beside them that had to contain a precious dog or cat. A man stood up and waved his arms frantically to signal the approaching helicopter. He then crouched to try and shelter his family as the helicopter hovered directly above them, with the downwash from the rotors rippling the water and tearing leaves from nearby trees.

Frankie had done the most recent winch job so it was theoretically Nico's turn to be winched down, but this rescue was going to be difficult.

Dangerous.

The urge to protect someone she loved was strong enough to make her turn towards Nico, with both her fist and her eyebrows raised, as an invitation to give her the chance to take the risks instead.

He held her gaze and he looked…almost angry?

'Don't even think about it,' he growled. 'There's no way I'd let you go down there.'

'I trust you,' Frankie said quietly. 'You'd keep me safe.'

But Nico was already checking his harness and attaching the hook.

'I'll bring the mum up first,' he said. 'Then the kid. I'll need a bag to put that crate in and I'll try and bring that up with the dad.'

'Clear to winch,' Mozzie confirmed only a minute or two later.

It was Frankie's job to operate the winch and keep Nico safe and she'd never felt the responsibility quite this sharply. Keeping Nico safe meant everything…

When he'd touched down on the roof and unhooked himself from the winch, Frankie's heart stopped for a moment as he slipped and fell on the wet corrugated iron. He slid towards the flat part of the roof over the veranda, where waves of the dirty water were breaking onto the iron. Frankie watched in horror as it seemed as if he was going to slide into that water and potentially get swept away to vanish without a trace and she knew, in that dreadful moment, that her life would never be the same without Nico Romano in it.

Even if it was only as a friend and colleague.

Losing him would be unbearable.

He managed to stop his slide in time for only his boots to hit the water. Frankie and Mozzie hovered and watched as Nico obviously had trouble persuading the mother to be the first person taken to safety. Maybe he told her that it would be far less terrifying for her child to be taken up to the helicopter if they knew that their mum was already there, waiting for them. And maybe he let them know, in no uncertain terms, that there was only a limited amount of daylight left and the wind was rising so the longer they left this rescue, the harder it would become.

Frankie could see the woman was following directions and keeping her arms down as she got near the skid, attached to Nico's harness. He grabbed the handle to steady himself and then got one foot in the helicopter door and one securely on the skid. Frankie could then get the woman safely inside the cabin and it was time to get Nico down again.

He leaned away from the skid to put all his weight into his harness and all his trust in Frankie's skill.

She held his gaze for a heartbeat before beginning to lower him again.

I've got this, she told him silently. *I'll keep you safe.*

And she did. It took another thirty minutes to get a small, terrified boy, his dad and an equally terrified Jack Russell terrier on board and then Mozzie headed towards the nearest evacuation centre, which happened to be a community hall close to Willhua hospital.

By all the rules set in place at the start of this frantic day, they should have gone straight back to base to stand down because they were already well over their allocated active time slot. But Frankie had been listening in mounting concern to an exchange on the radio that involved her friend Jenny. Apparently, when an ambulance was unable to reach a woman trapped by the floods who was in labour, she had kayaked in to the isolated farmhouse. She'd been there for hours and needed medical assistance for what she thought might become an obstetric emergency of an obstructed labour—a far more challenging situation than she and Nico had faced with the baby they'd delivered recently themselves.

Frankie came up with a solution and Mozzie was just as keen to break the rules.

'It won't take long,' he said. 'And it's our

Jen we're talking about. We can't leave her in trouble. If that's okay with you, Nico?'

Frankie knew the look that she gave Nico was a very heartfelt plea and she'd never loved him more than when he smiled back at her. A smile that told her he understood exactly how important this was to her. That said he would help her try to reach for the moon, if that was what she wanted to do this much.

A smile that made her think that Nico did really care about her. Love her, even if he didn't realise it?

'Of course it is,' was all he said.

So Frankie left Nico to carry the little boy on one hip and the dog crate in his other hand, leading the parents away from the aircraft towards the waiting volunteers ready to take them into the hall and care for them. She ran into the hospital, relieved to find someone right at the entrance. Had he been watching the helicopter land?

'You're Dr Pierson, right?' Rob Pierson—the man that Jenny was so keen on?

'Right.'

'I'm Frankie. South Sydney Air Rescue. Friend of Jen's.' Frankie was speaking rapidly but there was no time to waste. She filled him in on Jenny's predicament and the fact that they were beyond their time allowance to take on the job themselves but they were prepared to push boundaries enough to get Jenny the extra medical help she needed.

'I'd have to take you down, in a harness attached to mine, but I'll make sure you're safe. Could you come?'

Frankie understood at least a part of why Rob Pierson agreed to take on the mission, despite being warned of the risks involved, because she'd seen his face when she'd told him that Jenny had put herself in danger to help someone else. She'd probably looked like that herself in that horrible moment when she'd faced the thought of losing Nico. Was her imagination running wild, or was this another man who might care enough to be in love, even if he didn't realise it himself yet?

She had to admire the man's courage even more when they arrived at the scene. It was dark now and the only safe place to put Rob down was a small patch of dry land now illuminated by the night sun beneath the helicopter.

'We're ready to move to the door.' Frankie checked the carabiner that attached Rob's harness to her own. 'You want me to go through things one more time?'

'No. I have it.'

'You're sure?'

'I'm sure.'

It took only minutes to take Rob and his gear down, unhook him and take the harness back and then Nico was operating the winch to bring Frankie back on board. She could see him waiting for her, a dark shape in the door of the helicopter as she came up through the blindingly bright light of the night sun, and all Frankie could think about was how this reminded her of the first time he'd winched her. When her arms were full of his now-beloved dog. When he'd promised to keep her safe…

Such a short time ago.

But her life was never going to be the same. And, even if this all ended in tears, she wouldn't have wanted to miss a moment of it.

They were totally exhausted by the time they arrived back on base.

'Go home. Get some sleep,' Colin ordered. 'The forecast's looking better for tomorrow, but even if the rain stops completely and the water starts receding we're going to be in for a majorly increased workload with the massive clean-up and restricted access. Unless it's impossible, I'm going to make sure you both get at least a day off tomorrow.'

'Has Bruce been okay?' Nico rubbed at his eyes, which felt gritty with fatigue.

'Sorry, mate, I haven't heard. I don't think anyone's had the chance to get out there for a while.'

Frankie kept up with his long strides towards the van but Nico could only think about Bruce. How long had he been shut in the van? Had he been without food or water or a toilet break? Did he think he'd been abandoned?

He certainly looked as if he was desperate to get to the grass at the edge of the car park. Nico let him go, knowing his favourite tree that he always used. He leaned inside the van to check that the water dish wasn't dry and that no accidents had occurred from being shut inside for too long.

And then he heard Frankie shouting. She was angry and her words were almost a shriek.

'*Bruce... No...* You stupid, *stupid* dog...'

Nico's blood ran cold. That tone. That abusive language. It wasn't Frankie he was listening to now.

It was a ghost from his past.

Sofia.

He wasn't the one who was about to suffer pain and humiliation, but it was someone he loved very much. Someone who depended on him for protection.

Bruce.

He couldn't let this happen. Nico took off, running towards the grassed area on the edge of the car park. Shouting at Frankie. Swearing at her, even. Telling her to get the hell away from his dog.

Good grief...

Mr Perfect had morphed into someone Frankie couldn't recognise. An angry man who was shouting at her as if she was doing something absolutely unforgivable.

She was not only shocked, Frankie was frightened.

So she defended herself. And shouted back.

'He was about to run onto the road. He could have been killed. If you'd been looking after your dog I wouldn't have had to go anywhere near him.'

'You could have tried calling him. But you had to shout at him? *Hit* him?'

Frankie's indrawn breath was a gasp. 'I never *hit* him. I grabbed his collar, that's all.'

'I heard him howl.'

'So he got a fright. So did I, Nico.' But Frankie's anger was changing into something deeper. Something chilling. 'You *really* think I'd hit a dog? Any dog, let alone Bruce? Do I look like someone who would hurt anything on purpose?'

Nico was leaning down towards Bruce, who was looking as frightened as the first time Frankie had seen him, huddled on that cliff side near the wreck of that farm truck. 'As if you can tell what someone is capable of from the way they look,' he muttered. He was rubbing his dog's ears. 'It's okay, Bruce,' he said, his tone a world away from the one he'd just been using on Frankie. 'Everything's okay. Let's go home...'

It was a caring tone. Letting the dog know that he was loved. That he was going to be cared for. And Nico was walking away from Frankie without even a backwards glance.

How could she have almost convinced herself that Nico might be in love with her without realising it? He'd just attacked her verbally. Without even giving her a chance to defend herself. And now he was walking away?

It felt like history was repeating itself, with a twist she would never have seen coming. Maybe she was overreacting, but this had happened too many times before and it felt like it was happening again, even if, instead of another woman, Nico was choosing a relationship with a dog as more important than any connection he had with her.

Okay…she'd known it wasn't going to last, but hadn't they agreed that, when it ended, they would remain friends so that they could continue working together? This wasn't how friends treated each other and Frankie's heart was breaking.

She wasn't going to cry, though. Not here. Not in front of Nico.

So she tried to tap back into that anger of being accused of something she would never have done. The hurt that he would even think she was capable of doing.

'Nico?' Frankie knew her tone was an accusation. Had he not even heard her explanation? Was he not going to offer any kind of apology?

'Leave it, Frankie.' Nico still didn't turn around. He raised both his hands in the air in a gesture that could have been surrender. Or a warning not to come any closer? 'I don't want to talk about it.'

He sounded beyond exhausted.

Well, Frankie was exhausted too. And hurt. Something huge had just broken, in an unexpected and spectacular meltdown. and she couldn't make sense of how or why it had happened so suddenly.

Pushing Nico to keep talking now might only make things worse. It could take away any chance of repairing the damage. This was the downside of passion, wasn't it? A fight that was on the opposite side of the coin that had taught her just how amazing sex could be.

They both needed to sleep.

To calm down.

They might laugh about this one day. They might even say that it had been worth it because the make-up sex had been *so* good.

But Frankie couldn't even muster the hint of a smile right now. Or find a scrap of hope in the adage that tomorrow was another day and everything might look very different.

She could, instead, feel the first of what she knew might be many, many tears rolling down the side of her nose as she turned away.

CHAPTER TEN

TRUE TO HIS WORD, the base manager, Colin, stood Red Watch down to have a day's rest. The rain had stopped and there were patches of sunshine breaking through the cloud cover, but the enormous relief felt around the region was tempered by the continuous news coverage of people who were devastated by losing loved ones or who'd had their lives turned upside down, with homes and treasured possessions destroyed and pets missing, feared dead.

Frankie turned the news off. Despite utter exhaustion, she'd barely slept last night and couldn't face any more images of people stunned by the blow life had just dealt them. Her own heart felt as heavy as if she'd lost something tangible as well, but that only made her feel worse because she had no right to feel that way, did she?

In an effort to shake it off, Frankie put on

her sports top and shorts and tied up the laces of her well-worn trainers and set off for a run, hoping that a few endorphins might make her feel at least slightly more awake if they weren't up to the task of lifting her mood.

Without thinking, she took her normal route towards and then through the reserve, and maybe she'd been running faster than usual or it was the fatigue was dragging her down and making it much harder than it should have been. Whatever it was, Frankie needed to stop for a second to catch her breath. It wasn't until she was leaning forward, with her hands on her knees, that she realised she'd stopped in the spot where she could see that tiny beach where she'd spotted Bruce sitting, waiting for Nico.

The evening of their first kiss.

The evening where an irresistible attraction had exploded into an encounter so passionate—so *different*—that Frankie's life was never going to be the same.

Just this once…

She'd known, right from that first time, that it was never going to become something significant. What she hadn't known was that falling in love with someone wasn't something that could be controlled. Maybe if you turned your back on it and walked away before anything had started, you might be able to stop yourself falling over that cliff, but that wasn't what Frankie had done, was it?

No...she'd done the exact opposite. She might as well have taken a running jump and hurled herself willingly over that cliff.

Had she, deep down, known that it couldn't be controlled? Had that given her hope that Nico might fall in love with her, even when he'd been perfectly open about never wanting a committed relationship again? Had she believed that she might be 'the one' who could dissolve the barriers he had around his heart?

Finally, Frankie felt like she was dragging enough oxygen into her lungs and she raised her head as she straightened. Her gaze caught the curve of the small beach again, but there was no loyal dog sitting on the sand, waiting. There was, however, a pair of shoes on top of a towel and, when Frankie looked out onto the water, she could see the solitary figure of a man on the paddleboard in the distance, with the silhouette of a large dog, sitting proudly upright on the front of the board.

The board was moving swiftly through calm water. Even from this distance, Frankie could sense the power coming from Nico's muscles. The effort he was putting into his paddling. As if he was trying to get away from something?

It reminded her, with a sharp pang, of the way Nico had put his hands up last night to create a barrier to prevent her trying to get any closer. He hadn't wanted to talk to her then and it was obvious he didn't want to talk to anyone right now either. This was a man seeking solitude.

A lone wolf.

With his dog.

The thought should have been enough to make Frankie smile but, instead, she could feel the sting of tears that she'd thought had run completely dry in the early hours of this morning.

She pushed herself to start running again.

If Nico needed to be alone right now, she could let him have that space.

Because, if you loved someone enough, you could put their needs ahead of your own?

Nico could feel the burn.

The muscles in his shoulders were about to go on strike unless he slowed down and his legs ached from keeping his balance, but he didn't want to stop. The pain was welcome, in fact, because it was providing a very effective distraction. If the pain wasn't there, he'd have to start thinking about something else.

About the way he'd overreacted last night, perhaps. Or the fact that he needed to apologise to Frankie.

And if he did that he'd have to explain why it had happened. He'd end up telling her the whole story, and he didn't want to do that. He never wanted to do that. Because she'd think less of him, and the shame of that would be unbearable. He'd managed to avoid it for so long now, it felt like he'd left it completely behind. That he'd never have to face even a look from someone that would have said what he'd known they would all think.

You just stood there and let it happen to you? What kind of man are you...?

A man with no self-respect, that's who. No kind of man at all... You're pathetic... That's why it happened in the first place...

She was right, your wife...it was your fault she was so unhappy. So angry...

No wonder you didn't want anyone to know...

No wonder you ran away...

You'll be running away for the rest of your life. Because that's how pathetic you are...

Nico paddled harder but he'd turned back to shore now because, if he'd kept going the way he was, he would have ended up right out to sea and that would have been dangerous—for Bruce even more than for himself—and the need to protect this beloved companion of his was strong enough to override anything else right now.

It was also a reminder that he needed to do more than apologise to Frankie. That his dog was sitting here on his board right now was quite probably due to the fact that she'd saved his life last night by stopping him getting anywhere near the traffic. Poor Bruce had been so excited to be released from the confinement of the van that he probably hadn't even noticed the direction he was running in.

How devastating would it have been to lose this companion that had become such an important part of his life? It had been thanks to Frankie that he had come home with Nico in the first place. She was the one who'd risked her own safety to get a large dog into a harness on the side of a cliff and get him up to the helicopter. The first day they'd ever worked together.

Bruce was a part of *their* story as much as he was now a part of Nico's life that he couldn't imagine being without. Okay, it was clearly past time for him to step back from being Frankie's lover, but hadn't they agreed that when that happened they'd stay friends and be able to work together? He was the one who was putting that at risk.

So he was the one who needed to do something about it.

'How 'bout we go for a walk later, Bruce?' he suggested aloud. 'We could walk around to Frankie's house. Just to say hello.'

And thank you.

And, somehow, to say sorry. Even if it meant telling her something that could change the way she felt about him for ever.

'Sorry, mate...she's not here. She took off for a bike ride.'

'Do you know when she might be back?'

Derek shook his head. 'No idea. Could be a while. I think she likes to blow the cobwebs away by stretching out on the open road sometimes. Sounds like you guys had a pretty rough day yesterday?'

Nico nodded. It *had* been a rough day. Not only because of the dangerous conditions and relentless workload but because it had ended on such a bad personal note. Finding Frankie wasn't at home and her housemates didn't have any idea when she might return felt like any window of opportunity for repairing the

damage that had been done to their friendship was rapidly closing.

Frankie had every right to be angry with
him.

And Nico had learned a very long time ago
that it was a mistake to push an angry person into a conversation they were not ready
to have. If she needed the time to go and ride
that powerful motorbike as fast as possible
in order to clear her head, there was nothing
he could do about that.

Except hope like hell that she kept herself
safe…

And that they could find a quiet moment
at work tomorrow to put things right. Or to at
least get a signal that they *could* be put right.
Even a split second of connection would be
enough. Like the way they could decide who
took the lead in an assessment with an almost
invisible game of rock, paper, scissors?

They had to run to get straight on board the
helicopter within minutes of arriving for the
shift the next day to respond to a Priority
One call-out.

Frankie didn't even look to see if Nico
wanted to play the deciding game. She had
carefully avoided making eye contact as well.
Because she couldn't afford to make this any

harder than it already was. Derek had told her that Nico and Bruce had come to the house yesterday and she had guessed that he wanted to apologise. He'd probably wanted to confirm that their fling was over but suggest that they could still be friends and work well together.

She wasn't ready to talk about that.

It wasn't as if they had any choice about whether or not they kept working together right now. Maybe it was just as well that they were likely to get hammered with callouts today. Along with the urgent missions to trauma or medical cases like this first job, there was still a waiting list of people needing evacuation from inaccessible areas and much-needed supplies that were being delivered to rural emergency services and more remote medical centres and hospitals.

It wasn't raining again yet but there was a heavy cloud cover which made everything grey and gloomy and there was still an ocean of dirty water beneath them and rivers that were angry torrents. The rising wind and the unexpected gusts that were jolting the aircraft meant that Mozzie was concentrating on his flying to the extent he probably didn't notice the lack of any conversation that wasn't

strictly professional in the cabin of his helicopter.

Frankie could see where water levels had
fallen in the small town they were flying
over. Now there were piles of debris growing
on mud-covered streets. Carpets were being
pulled up and ruined furniture and fabrics
moved to where they would be collected and
disposed of. That was what the patient they
were being called to see had been doing. He'd
been dragging a mattress from a bed upstairs
in his house and had fallen through sodden
floorboards, hitting his head on an exposed
brick chimney on the way.

It was a relief to know that Nico was as focused as she was on what lay ahead.

'He was knocked out but has now regained
consciousness.' Nico was reading an update
on his tablet. 'He's communicating but confused and has a laceration on his head that a
local first responder's keeping pressure on.'

'The nearest hospital with neurosurgical
and neuro intensive care facilities is going to
be St Mary's. That's more than a ten-minute
transport time.'

Which meant that intubating this patient
would be a priority if his oxygen levels were
too low or his level of consciousness was
dropping. There were special considerations

with a severe traumatic brain injury for maintaining a higher blood pressure and which drugs to use. Frankie spent a few seconds reminding herself of how to calculate a mean arterial pressure by adding the systolic pressure to twice the diastolic pressure and then dividing the sum by three. Nico looked as if he was doing something similar.

Yeah…it was a good thing that they had no choice about whether or not they worked together for now. This shared passion for their work and that ability they'd had right from the start to put anything personal aside might be exactly what was going to help Frankie deal with what felt like a bit of a disaster in her personal life. It might make her a better person, even. And being able to continue working with Nico would certainly make her a better paramedic.

Gerald, their sixty-eight-year-old patient, was lying amidst the carnage in his home that advertised a life in ruins, with sodden photograph albums and broken family treasures amongst the mud, and things had just got a whole lot worse for both Gerald and his family. His level of consciousness had dropped by the time the air rescue team arrived. He could open his eyes when asked to but he was only groaning rather than talking and wasn't following commands but only pulling away from something painful.

'GCS of eight,' Frankie estimated. It was a significant drop from the score of thirteen the local paramedic had given on arrival.

'And he's hypoxic.' Nico had clipped the saturation monitor to Gerald's finger. 'His oxygen level is below ninety percent. Let's get a non-rebreather mask on and, if that's not enough to get it up to at least ninety-five percent, he'll need some help with a bag valve mask before we secure his airway. Are you okay to cover that while I get an IV line in?'

Frankie was already attaching a mask to an oxygen cylinder. Getting Gerald's oxygen saturation up to more normal levels was the most important thing they could do to try and prevent the catastrophic brain damage that could result from an inadequate oxygen supply. They also had to try and get his blood pressure high enough to keep that oxygen circulating.

They hadn't needed to decide who was taking the lead in this case because their ability to work together seamlessly was still there. The minutes flew past as they worked to stabilise Gerald and try to minimise the effect that this serious injury was going to have on his future.

'I'm not happy with that level of oxygenation yet. The fluids are improving blood pressure but his saturation's still too low.'

'I agree.'

'The longer we put off intubation, the more hypoxic he's going to get.'

'Gerald?' Frankie leaned down so that her mouth was close to his ear. 'Can you open your eyes for me?'

There was no response.

'GSC is dropping.' Nico nodded. 'Let's get on with this.' He turned to the local paramedic. 'We need to clear any unnecessary gear to give us some space. Bring that suction unit closer and check that it's working.' He opened his drug kit and reached for syringes and ampoules of the medications needed to sedate and paralyse their patient.

Frankie hooked some nasal prongs around Gerald's ears but kept using the mask to pre-oxygenate him, trying to get his levels up enough to get him through the inevitable period when it would not be possible to supplement his oxygen while the tube was being placed in his trachea. She used rolled-up towels and a damp but serviceable pillow to put his head into the best position, with his ear in line with his sternal notch.

It was Nico who administered the drugs

and then moved swiftly to insert the laryngoscope and the tube that would keep the airway safe for transport. Frankie was ready with the device to secure the tube in place, the ventilation bag with a PEEP valve attached and a stethoscope to hand to Nico so that he could check that the tube was in the right place.

It was. They both watched the lungs rise evenly when Frankie squeezed the bag and they both looked up to catch each other's gaze, their heads close together because they were both so intent on what they were doing.

And maybe the way Frankie found herself pulling in a deep breath was not just because they were over the first hurdle in getting this patient safely to the care he needed at St Mary's but because it felt just as natural as it always did when they were working together.

Nothing had changed. Professionally, anyway, and that had to be a good thing.

There were plenty of willing volunteers to help carry the stretcher to where Mozzie was waiting with the helicopter on the only recognisable patch of the town's rugby field.

There were more than just emergency department personnel waiting for them on the roof of St Mary's. Frankie's eyebrows rose as she saw a second stretcher being wheeled in their direction. She looked around but couldn't see another rescue helicopter waiting its turn to land.

'Didn't want to disturb you guys when you were so busy in the back,' Mozzie told her. 'We've been asked to take some gear to a rural hospital down south. They're low on dressings, splints and drugs. They've asked for backup defibrillator batteries and a charger as well. The local volunteer ambulance crew has borrowed the only ones they have. Shouldn't take too long. The main street's cleared for landing for us and someone will be waiting.'

'No worries.'

Both Nico and Frankie helped to load and secure the supplies in the back of the helicopter. There were enough of them to create a kind of wall between them and that felt like another small respite from an inevitable moment with Nico, when they couldn't shelter behind their professional relationship and had to face how much everything had changed between them on a personal basis. It was also kind of helpful that a rain squall was giving them a bit of turbulence. Frankie stared out of the window on her side, watching the ground beneath them get blurred by the sudden rain and not breaking the silence.

Until she saw something.

'Did you see that? In the river?'

'See what?'

'I thought I saw something white.' Oh, help…was Nico thinking the same thing that had just flashed through the back of her mind? That she'd said something very similar when she'd spotted where Bruce had been hidden on that cliff. Was she going to be ambushed by memories of their brief time together for the rest of her life?

'Something big,' she added hurriedly. 'It could have been the roof of a car…'

Mozzie was turning and the helicopter rocked with the gust of wind from the change of direction in the squally weather. 'Let's go back and take a quick look,' he said calmly.

This river was wide—a huge ribbon of brown water moving swiftly enough to create foaming waves around the edges of any debris caught in its path, like the huge island of tree trunks and branches that had accumulated around the remains of a washed-out bridge. Mozzie started there and flew upriver towards where they'd been a minute ago, but low enough now to be able to see just how fast this water was moving.

'Can't see anything,' Frankie said. 'Sorry…'

'It could well have been washed away by now. Or be underwater.'

'We'll go downriver—just for a kilometre or two. It might be caught on that wrecked bridge.'

Mozzie turned the helicopter again but, as he did so, Frankie could feel the tail of the helicopter swing unexpectedly. She could actually feel the wind shear that was not only moving them horizontally but vertically. She knew they were probably too close to ground level for Mozzie to be able to correct for the sudden change in wind direction and velocity and she knew they were in trouble, but it all happened too fast for Mozzie to give them any warning. Too fast for Frankie to be terrified, even.

One instant they were flying above the river.

And the next they nosedived into the water at a speed that sent them below the surface to tip and roll as they were swept along in the current. Anything that hadn't been firmly secured in the cabin was now a danger and Frankie put her arms up over her face to protect herself from the boxes and plastic containers that were jolted free of the wall that had been between herself and Nico. She closed her eyes and waited then, because what was running through her mind with astonishing speed in those moments were the crash survival rules that had been drummed into all the participants during the classroom sessions of survival training.

Do not attempt to leave the aircraft until all movement has ceased.

Maintain orientation. Where is the door?

If in water, wait until all bubbles have cleared.

Let the aircraft fill with water. The door cannot be opened when it's under water pressure from the outside.

Release your harness. Open the door. Escape...

Frankie's thoughts were abruptly interrupted because they hit something.

Something solid enough to have stopped any movement of the fuselage. Was it one of the bridge supports amongst that island of debris?

It was quite likely to have been a big tree branch that had smashed the bubble windscreen of the helicopter and, as the cabin began to rapidly fill with water, Frankie could see Mozzie struggling to release his harness. She saw him try to get a hand grip to turn and look back, but he was already being pulled through the shattered windscreen and into the current of the river and he disappeared almost instantly.

With that wall of supplies they'd been due to deliver now scattered and being dragged towards the front of the helicopter, Frankie could see, despite rapidly deteriorating visibility with water splashing on her visor and the darkness of whatever was surrounding them in the water, that Nico was trying to do what she was doing and release the clips on his harness.

They'd both done a HUET course—Helicopter Underwater Escape Training— where a specially designed deep swimming pool had a crane beside it that could raise and lower a metal cage that simulated the structure of a helicopter and its seating and door positions. Frankie had done a refresher course not long ago and it had been more advanced than the initial introduction, where she'd only been taught to escape a helicopter after it had been partially submerged and still vertical in the water and then again with the position changed to mimic an aircraft tipped onto its side. On this new course, she'd had the rather terrifying experience of being flipped upside down and then submerged, with a follow-up of doing it again wearing blackout goggles.

At least this hadn't happened at night or out at sea. And, even though they had been tipped and rolled, they had ended up not being fully upside down. But this was fast moving, dirty water around them and, although it felt like they were securely wedged and not about to start moving again any time soon, this was an alarmingly dangerous situation and...

And Nico was trying to get himself free with only one arm.

His other arm looked as if it was twisted and trapped between bent or broken parts of both the fuselage and the back of his seat.

Frankie was free now. She knew she had to make sure she maintained her orientation so that she knew exactly where the door was. She took a deep breath in the diminishing space that had any air available, but she was holding on tight to the handles and other solid structures. They were more protected from the current of the river in the cabin than Mozzie had been when the windscreen shattered but she wasn't going to risk being sucked in a direction she didn't want to go yet.

She wanted to go towards Nico.

Because it hadn't even occurred to Frankie to leave him behind in order to save herself.

CHAPTER ELEVEN

FEAR WAS BEING kept at bay by a level of determination to survive that was so powerful it made Frankie feel like she was capable of anything.

Even getting the door open, which took a great deal of physical strength.

Something else from that survival course was surfacing in her brain as she slid the door sideways. She'd been told that a big part of survival was a matter of this kind of determination. People could—and did—survive in the face of seemingly impossible challenges and her instructor had suggested that the real killers could be fear, a lack of confidence and an inability to problem solve.

Frankie wasn't lacking any of those factors. She'd decided to open the side door because that would give them an easier, faster exit than getting to the front of the helicopter to go out of the broken windscreen. She had already used the shears attached to her tool belt to hack through the safety harness where it was caught up in the gap where Nico's arm was trapped almost to his elbow and she thought he'd be able to pull himself free while she wrestled the door open.

The last space in the cabin was filling with water so time was running out. How long could she hold her breath?

More or less than a minute?

How much was physical effort going to reduce that time limit by?

Nico was still trapped but his position was awkward enough to affect how hard he could pull. Frankie took hold of his arm with both hands to increase the force of the pressure but his arm didn't budge. And she could hear his cry of pain even underwater. He cut it short but even that must have stolen too much of the precious oxygen he was holding in his lungs.

Claws of fear were hooking themselves into Frankie.

For a tiny flicker of time that would haunt her for ever, she was convinced they were both going to die. Amazingly, even in the face of that fear there was something like… what was it…gratitude that she was with Nico? That her last moment of consciousness could be the awareness that she was with the man she loved *this* much?

And was it simply that Nico's eyes were a mirror for what had to be showing in her own?

No. Frankie might have been convinced that they were both about to die, but she was even more convinced that what she could see in Nico's eyes was a love for her that was just as powerful as the way she felt about him.

And that suddenly changed everything.

Frankie was not going to give up. She was going to fight to the end with everything she had. The fresh burst of adrenaline, or determination or whatever it was, gave her a strength she had no idea she possessed. She braced herself as she gripped Nico's arm again and when she pulled this time it was hard enough for her to feel a bone snapping beneath her hands, but even that sickening sensation only made her more determined.

Stronger.

And she could feel the movement. Breaking that bone had made it possible to change the angle of Nico's hand and wrist within whatever obstacle had trapped him, but she could feel him slumping as she pulled him clear. Frankie had to find even more strength to drag him towards the open door and then she had to try and use the last seconds of her own consciousness to remember which way she had to take them both to get to the surface of this water.

Which way was up?

Thank goodness she'd paid so much attention to that course because the final flashback might be the one that could save them both.

Blow out a breath. Bubbles always rise. Follow the bubbles...

So Frankie blew out the air she'd been holding in her lungs so long they felt ready to explode. And then, holding onto Nico as tightly as she could, she braced her feet against the fuselage of the helicopter and pushed hard enough to send them both into, but also up, through the swirling current of the deadly river.

She felt her head breaking the surface and tried to pull Nico's face clear of the water at the same time she was dragging in her first, painful gasp of air. She could feel her strength fading, however. There was no way she could keep them both above water if they got swept downriver. But staying where they were still meant they were in extreme danger. They could be hit at any second by another huge lump of debris.

But it felt as if natural forces were on their side now. The turbulent swirls and waves of the river surface were turning them, pushing them past the bent tip of a rotor blade showing above the surface and towards the island of tangled branches and tree trunks caught on the remains of the bridge structure. Some of the boxes and containers from the helicopter had added themselves to the mix and, although the small items were moving and some were getting sucked free, the rest of this artificial island felt more than solid enough to climb onto.

Best of all, Nico was conscious enough to help drag himself onto the pile. Pretty much inside it, in fact, because there was a kind of cave where huge pieces of this debris had crossed and caught and then other pieces had woven themselves around and over them. It was dense enough to cut a surprising amount of the noise from the rushing water outside and high enough to be out of range of the foaming waves of the rapids. Frankie had no idea how stable it might actually be but, for now, it felt safe. Solid. She was alive.

So was Nico...

He was sitting beside her, still dragging air into his lungs, and Frankie still hadn't let go of the tight hold she had on him.

She couldn't.

All Frankie could do was burst into tears.

'I broke your arm,' she sobbed. 'I'm *so* sorry, Nico.'

'It doesn't matter.' Nico's voice sounded raw. 'You saved my life, Frankie…'

He was holding her now, as tightly as Frankie was holding him. She might have got Nico out of the helicopter but they weren't out of the woods yet. What if this pile of debris broke apart and they were dragged back into the current and washed away? Like Mozzie had been?

Oh…there was an unbearable grief laced into that thought that Frankie couldn't afford to acknowledge yet. There was too much to try and deal with already. Too much to be frightened by. What if no one found them and they died of hypothermia? They were already wet and cold. The shelter of this odd cave might not be enough to save them, even if they were holding each other like this. Which had to be hurting Nico's arm.

But it *did* matter that she'd broken Nico's arm.

Frankie lifted her head so that she could look directly at Nico. She still had tears streaming down her face. 'I would never want to hurt you, Nico. How could I? I *love* you… I love you *so* much…'

Oh, God… Was that just river water trickling from inside his helmet or had she made Nico cry now? Because it was the last thing he wanted to hear her say?

'You didn't hurt me because you wanted to,' he said. 'You did it because you wanted to save me.'

Frankie nodded. 'Because I love you…' She pulled herself away from Nico, rubbing at her eyes to clear her blurred vision. 'And now I need to look after you. Let me see your arm.'

She must have dropped her shears when she'd hacked through that harness but the sleeve of Nico's flight suit was shredded anyway so she didn't need to cut his clothing clear to examine his arm. The skin around his forearm was grazed and, no doubt, badly bruised but it was the deformity in the bones of his wrist that was obviously the most serious injury. It was a classic fracture of the distal radius close to the wrist, with a dorsal angulation. A Colles fracture, often called a 'dinner fork' fracture because of the shape it made.

'Can you move your fingers? Can you feel me touching them?'

'I think so…yes…a little.' The grimace Nico made advertised how painful it was.

'It's impossible to assess your skin colour or capillary refill when you're this cold. I can hardly feel your radial pulse…'

'I'm alive. It's all good.' Nico was actually smiling at her and Frankie had to catch her breath and try to focus on what she was doing.

'Can you move your elbow?'

'Yes.'

'Does it hurt?'

'No.'

'I need to splint this arm.' Frankie looked around her. 'I wonder if there's anything useful in those boxes.' She had something positive to focus on now, and her mind was starting to feel like it was functioning properly again. 'I'm going to have a look. Don't move, Nico. And hold onto your arm.' She gently bent the broken limb so that it was across his chest and put his other hand close to the elbow to keep it still.

She found bandages and dressings in the first box she reached. They were completely sodden but they would still be useful. The cardboard, which could have made a great splint if it had been dry, was totally useless. But there were any number of branches around her and it wasn't hard to find some that were small enough to snap. The sound and feel of breaking them was a nasty reminder of how it had felt to break Nico's arm but she knew he was right. He wouldn't be alive now if she hadn't done something that dramatic. Neither of them would be, because she wouldn't have left him to die alone.

She made a ball out of wet gauze and put it in the palm of Nico's hand so that his fingers had support and wouldn't move and cause more pain and potentially more damage to any nerves or blood vessels affected by the fracture. She put sticks on either side of his arm from his elbow to beyond his fingers, holding them in place with one hand while she used her teeth to rip open the plastic covering of a crepe bandage so that she could bind the sticks together. She opened another bandage to secure Nico's arm across his body for even more support.

'Is that okay?'

'It's great. *Ben fatto, cara.*'

The praise for a job well done was heartbreaking, given that she had caused the injury herself, but Nico was smiling at her and Frankie could feel her face crumpling into lines that felt like...

Pure love, that was what it felt like.

And gratitude, that she'd allowed herself to break those stupid rules about both Italian men and the people she worked with. If she hadn't, she might never have discovered that a love like this actually existed. Something so huge, so astonishingly wonderful, that anything else in life was in the shadow of how brightly it shone.

It didn't feel like simply a reflection of what she was feeling that she could see in Nico's eyes this time. It felt like she was seeing a part of Nico she'd never been allowed to see before. Frankie knew, deep down, even if he never said anything, that Nico loved her and, weirdly, in the most dangerous situation she'd ever been in, Frankie had the sensation of feeling *safer* than she ever had before.

'*Dai, andiamo...*'

Let's go? Frankie's smile wobbled. They couldn't go anywhere, could they? Their only chance of survival was to stay on this temporary refuge of the debris island and hope like hell that they would get rescued.

'Are you sure your arm's feeling okay? That bandage isn't too tight, is it?'

'It's fine, *cara.*'

'I should have asked already, but have you ever fractured this arm before?'

Nico nodded. Frankie touched the top of

his arm where it was exposed by the shredded sleeve of the flight suit and touched her fingers to the patch of rippled, damaged skin. A touch that sparked a kaleidoscope of memories and sensations and emotions that had been there every time they'd made love.

Because that was what it had been, right from the start, even though Frankie would have denied that as fiercely as Nico would have. It had never been simply about the sex, had it?

Nico's scars were like a physical form of the barrier that had been erected to hide what was really going on. The stories about how he'd got the scars were there as reinforcements. Frankie had respected those barriers, but what was the point of them now? What if this was the last time they would ever be together?

'Was it when you did this?' She tried to find her smile again. 'The mountain biking accident? Or when the shark bit you?'

Nico shook his head again. Slowly. 'There was never a shark,' he admitted.

'I knew that.' Frankie was still doing her best to smile but Nico was holding her gaze and she felt a sudden chill run down her spine. 'You got burnt, didn't you? And it wasn't an exploding skyrocket.'

'No. I got too close to an iron.'

'And what was it that broke your arm the first time?'

'It got slammed in a door,' Nico said.

Nico had closed his eyes. Frankie could see the deep breath he dragged in. 'It's not the *what* that's the important thing,' he said. 'It's the *who*.' He opened his eyes to catch Frankie's gaze directly. 'It was Sofia who broke my arm. Who used the iron to burn me. Who did so many things to hurt me.'

There was nothing left of Frankie's smile. It felt like the blood was draining from her face. Making it freeze so that it was hard to move her lips. 'Who's Sofia?'

'She was my wife.'

There…

He'd said it.

In the craziest of situations, when it was still possible they weren't going to survive this and he could have taken his shameful secret to his grave, but the words had come out. He'd almost had to shout them, over the roar of the river around them and the crash of new debris that shook the small hole they'd found to hide in and…and it had almost felt like a cry of victory.

Of freedom.

He had to do it.

Because Frankie loved him.

Because she had risked her own life to save his.

But, most of all, because *he* loved *her*. Because he knew he could not only trust her with his life, he could trust her with his heart and soul. He could trust her not to ever want to hurt him. The complete opposite, in fact. He would never feel this safe with anybody else. Ever.

He'd known it all along. He just hadn't been brave enough to peel off that protective layer he'd encased himself in, so many years ago. Just in case that, if Frankie saw the truth, she wouldn't feel the same way about him.

Frankie was looking beyond shocked but, in a way, this was a good thing. She wasn't thinking about the danger they were still in. Or feeling scared that any rescue attempt might come too late. What Nico didn't want, however, was the mortification he could see filling her eyes. She had just broken his arm and she'd chosen to do it and, sure…it could have taken him back to that dark place of being in such an abusive relationship.

But it hadn't.

It had set him free.

'*Don't,*' he commanded. 'Don't ever think like that. I know you would never want to hurt anybody. Your whole life is about trying to stop people hurting. I knew you would never have hurt Bruce. I know you would never hurt me.' He touched Frankie's face with his fingers. 'I know you love me.'

Frankie's eyes were huge. So filled with emotion they looked black. 'How?' she asked. 'How do you know that?'

Nico touched his chest, just above where his splinted arm was secured across his body. Right over his heart.

'Because I can feel it,' he said. 'Here. And I know it's real because it feels the same as what's in here already. Because I love *you*, Frankie...'

Tears were spilling from those huge, dark eyes. 'I thought you might, but you never said anything so I couldn't tell you how *I* felt.'

'I couldn't say anything because I couldn't tell you the truth. I didn't want you to think it might have been because of how bad a husband I was.'

'Oh, my God... I know that's not true.' A poignant smile was breaking through those tears. 'I knew instantly how gentle and caring you are. I knew that from the moment I saw you holding Bruce in your arms for that ride back to base. I think that was the moment I started falling in love with you...'

Even with Frankie's great job of make-shift splinting, it hurt to use his good arm to pull her close but he couldn't have cared less. Nico had to kiss her. Because he'd seen the look in her eyes—that sheer amazement, followed by a kind of happiness that shouldn't have been possible given the danger they were in.

He'd also seen that the love was still there, even when he'd told her the worst about himself, and Nico could feel himself catching some of that joy, even though he was very aware of what was still threatening them. So aware that that kiss was fierce but only brief. He was monitoring the slightest movement in the pile of debris beneath them and the need to protect Frankie if it started breaking apart was paramount. If it was solid enough to support them until rescue came, it was the danger of hypothermia he needed to try and protect her from. All he could do was hold her as close as he could to his own body.

To wrap his arms—and his love—around her.

Frankie was still distracted from the danger. She almost sounded angry as she looked up at him again. Thanks to how dense this shelter they'd been lucky enough to find, he could hear her clearly when he bent his head.

'How long were you married for, Nico?'

'Too long,' he admitted. 'Five years. We were both too young but we were in love.'

Frankie shook her head. 'Nobody wants to hurt a person they love.'

'It wasn't like that at the beginning. I knew she had a bad temper. That she would shout and throw things and break them when she was angry. I thought the first time she hurt me had been an accident. I'd just got in the way of the broken bottle she threw. I wear my hair long to cover that scar.'

'Oh… *Nico*…' The pain in Frankie's voice made it crack. 'I don't understand how she could do that. How *anyone* could do that.'

'It didn't happen again for a long time, but then it did. And the more often it happened, the worse it got.'

'Didn't anybody else know?'

'I couldn't tell anyone.' Nico shook his head. 'You know how it is in Italy. The men are in control. If any hitting is done, it's done by the men. The *real* men.'

'No…' Frankie looked as fierce as she sounded. 'The *real* men are the ones who never do it in the first place. The ones who are strong enough to not hit back.' She was biting her bottom lip. 'How did you get away from her?'

'She said I couldn't leave. That she would tell everyone that I hurt *her* and she was only protecting herself. That I was stupid. The worst husband anyone could ever have... And then she would say how sorry she was. That she loved me. That she'd never do it again...'

'You were trapped...' The darkness in Frankie's eyes looked like anger.

'It was my sister Rosa who found out what was happening. I made her swear that she would keep it a secret and not go to the police, or even tell the rest of the family, but she would only do that if Sofia agreed to divorce me and disappear from my life. Sofia had no choice. My sister can be scary when she's protecting the people she loves.' He smiled at Frankie. 'Like you...' His heart felt like it was filling up to breaking point—in a good way.

'I'm scary?'

'I will never forget the expression on your face when you were fighting to get me free. You weren't going to give up, were you?'

Frankie's eyes were full of tears. 'Of course not. I felt like I was fighting for my own life as much as yours. I was so afraid I was going to lose you.'

'You'll never lose me,' Nico vowed. 'Because I give you my heart and you will have that for as long as you live, even if I'm not there to hold you... Like this...' He tightened his hold on Frankie, ignoring any pain in his arm.

'And mine is yours,' Frankie said. 'I didn't mean to give it to you because I knew you didn't want it, but...it happened anyway. I think it was always going to happen...'

'I want it,' Nico said. 'I've never wanted anything as much as I want to be loved by you. And to love you back. Except...'

Frankie's eyes widened. 'Except what?'

'I really, really want to get out of here.'

And in that moment, as if the universe had been eavesdropping on this extraordinary conversation, there was a steady thump, thump, thump of sound above the noise of the rushing water outside this woven cave. A sound that got quickly louder until it was right above Nico and Frankie.

Hovering...

He pulled himself away from Frankie. Maybe the locator beacon that would have gone off automatically when they'd crashed had brought rescuers to this exact point or perhaps the bright red of their flight suits could be seen through gaps in the tangle of debris but he wasn't about to take any chances.

'Stay there,' he commanded.

He scrambled out of their shelter and pulled himself upright to wave with his un-injured arm. He could see the side door of the helicopter was open and someone was in his favourite position, clipped to an overhead anchor but leaning out, with one foot on the skid to balance themselves as they searched for their target.

He got a 'thumbs-up' signal in return and another head appeared in the doorway. It was impossible to be sure, but he thought it might be Ricky. Whoever it was, the wide grin on his face made their delight in finding survivors very obvious. Both faces disappeared back into the cabin at that point, but Nico knew that they were getting ready to send someone down on the winch line with an extra harness to take them up. One at a time.

He crouched to crawl back into the cave.

'Dai, andiamo,' he shouted over the noise of the river and the helicopter. 'Let's go… Put your helmet on properly again. You're going up first.'

But Frankie didn't move. She raised her

eyebrows and held her hand up in a fist and Nico couldn't decide whether he needed to laugh or cry. She wanted to play rock, paper, scissors?

Maybe he needed to do both. But not yet. Not until he had the woman he loved so much in the safest place he could find.

'Not this time, *amore mio*,' he said. He held out his hand. 'This time it's my turn to look after you.'

CHAPTER TWELVE

'FRANKIE...OH, MY GOD... Colin didn't know where you'd been taken. I've rung every hospital in Sydney... How badly hurt are you? Can you talk? Why aren't you saying anything?'

'Because I can't get a word in?' Frankie gave a huff of laughter which hurt her ribs. She had bumps and bruises she hadn't even been aware of until she'd been brought into this emergency department to be thoroughly checked. 'I'm okay, Jen. So's Nico, thank goodness. Apart from a broken wrist which is being set for him right now in the fracture clinic.'

Jenny was crying now. 'And Ricky? What about Mozzie? I couldn't get through to anyone at the SSAR. Colin's message got relayed to me via Comms and they're overwhelmed by work. I couldn't keep pestering them.'

'Ricky wasn't with us. He was working

with another crew who turned out to be the ones that came to rescue us.'

'And Mozzie?'

Frankie was also crying. 'We were so sure he hadn't made it. I'd actually seen him get sucked out of the chopper as soon as he got his harness off. We weren't completely underwater then and the current was wild.' She took in a breath to stop her voice wobbling. 'But he got swept down rapids and around a bend and got spotted by an SES crew in an inflatable rescue boat. He's okay. He's up in the fracture clinic with Nico because he hurt his ankle but he got wheeled in to see us when we arrived. It was Mozzie who raised the alarm about the crash.'

'And you're sure you're okay?'

'I'm fine. Feeling exhausted but incredibly lucky to be alive.' Incredibly lucky in more ways than simply having survived, but there was all the time in the world to tell her best friend about what had happened between herself and Nico. For now, it was too amazing and new and life-changing to share. It was something precious and, huddled together in that short trip from the river to the closest hospital, it had seemed like they'd made a tacit agreement that they would keep it private as long as they could.

Because this was just between them.

Like the secret that Nico had shared with her because he knew he could trust her. Completely.

For ever.

'What about you, Jen? I haven't had the chance to talk to you since we dropped Rob in to help you when you were trapped with that woman in labour. Did things work out okay?'

'Couldn't have worked out better—and not just for the mum and her gorgeous baby, who are both safe and well.'

'What… You mean…?' Frankie could feel the corners of her mouth curling up.

'You were right. He is my Doc Pierson. My Rob…' The tone of Jenny's voice made it obvious that she was smiling too. 'I've found the person I want to be with for the rest of my life. You're not going to tell me it's too soon to know, are you?'

'No…' Through the gap in the curtain drawn around her bed, Frankie could see someone walking into the observation ward where she'd been left to rest, having been cleared of any major injury. Someone who had a cast on his arm and a way more professional-looking sling than a few loops of crepe bandage. 'I'm only going to tell you how very happy I am for you. But I need to go, Jen. Love you. Talk soon, yeah?'

'Oh, sorry…are you with someone?

But Frankie was already ending the call. She had put the cordless ward phone down on the locker beside her bed by the time Nico had come through the curtain and pulled it properly closed behind him.

Yes…

She was with someone.

She was going to be with him for the rest of her life.

She couldn't find any words to describe how happy she was feeling in this moment. All Frankie could do was to hold out her arms and invite Nico close enough to feel her heart beating. Close enough to give him the kind of kiss that might be able to let him know what she would say if she could find the right words.

'I need to go.' Reluctantly, Nico stood up after giving Frankie one last kiss. 'I got hold of Colin and he said Bruce is getting anxious. He's bringing some dry clothes from my locker and he's going to drive my van here to pick me up and then take us both home.'

'Both of us?' Frankie nodded. 'Is he bringing me some clothes too?'

'I think he meant me and Bruce.' But Nico was smiling. 'I could share my clothes with you, but there's only two seats in the front of the van.'

'So Colin can take a taxi back. I'll drive you. You need someone to keep an eye on you.' She was waving a hand in the air to emphasise her words. 'What if you've had a head injury they've missed? Bruce isn't going to be much help when you're lying on the floor unconscious, is he?'

Bossy Frankie was back. Talkative, loud and hand-waving Frankie was back. Normal life was resuming and Nico couldn't be happier about that.

It was never going to be the same life, of course. Too much had changed in the last few hours and Nico couldn't be happier about that either.

'I haven't got a head injury.' Nico leaned down to kiss Frankie again. 'And you need to rest. They want you to stay here overnight.'

'They want you to stay as well.'

'I can't. I have a fur child who needs me.'

Frankie couldn't argue with that but she was scowling.

'I'll come and get you in the morning,' Nico promised.

'With one arm? How?' Frankie was pushing back the blanket covering her and wriggling to get her legs over the side of the bed. 'Have you taught Bruce to drive?'

'No. But he's getting good at paddleboarding. Not that we'll be doing any of that for a while.' Nico was grinning now. He had a feeling he was losing this battle and he didn't actually mind at all. 'I think there's only one way to settle this argument, isn't there?'

Frankie's eyes lit up. 'You're on.' She stood up and held out a fist. 'One, two…three…'

They both kept a fist. The rock couldn't defeat another rock.

'Again,' Frankie ordered. 'One, two… three…'

They both had their middle and index fingers in a V shape. Scissors couldn't win over scissors.

They were holding each other's gaze as they tried for a third time. They both kept their hands flat. Paper was equal to paper.

They both laughed.

Frankie shook her head. 'Neither of us is going to win.'

But Nico smiled. 'I think it's because we've both already won, *amore mio*. We have each other.'

Frankie's smile was misty. 'I think you're right.'

She was leaning closer. Close enough for Nico to kiss her again and he was about to, when he saw the mischievous gleam in her eyes.

'So that means I can come home with you?'

'*Sì*…' Nico's lips were almost touching hers now. 'I don't want you to be anywhere else. Ever.'

'Good…' Frankie lips were brushing his so he could both hear and feel her murmured words. 'Neither do I.'

EPILOGUE

Three years later...

'BUDGE UP.'

'Budge up?' Rosa was laughing as she echoed Nico's command. *'Non capisco.'*

'I thought you wanted to speak English on your holiday. It means *spostati*. You need to move closer so I can get a photo of everybody to send home to the rest of the family.'

Rosa moved along the wooden bench on one side of the big table beneath the pergola that had a young grapevine doing its best to create some leafy shade in the Australian summer. She was close enough to put her arm around Frankie's shoulders and the sisters-in-law shared a fond smile. Rosa's husband, Giovanni, was encouraging their four children to gather and stand still but they were all performing in front of Nico.

'Take our photo,' they shouted. 'And when can we go to the beach again?'

'Don't ever go on holiday with children,' Rosa warned Frankie. 'It's total chaos.' And then she laughed again. 'Oops...too late.'

They were both still laughing as Nico took their photo, but Frankie wasn't looking at the camera. She had turned her head to look towards the end of the table, where her mother and *nonna* were sitting. Her *nonna* was holding the bundle that was her six-week-old son Paolo, who was the most perfect baby in the world. He even already looked like his *papà*.

Mr Perfect.

Not that anyone was perfect, of course, but this man that Frankie loved a little more with every extra day they got to spend together was as close as it got.

Their life was as close to perfect as anyone could hope for too.

They were still living in the little blue beach house that Nico had rented, but they owned it now and they were fixing it up and making it bigger when time and money allowed. One of the first things they'd done after they'd been lucky enough to buy the property was to build this outside courtyard with its paved floor and big, rustic wooden table and benches and the grapevine that would eventually make it a gorgeous, green outside room with lots of shade for summer.

Because this was a place for family to gather. The way the Romanos had in a similar courtyard when Frankie and Nico went back to Italy to get married nearly two years ago. The way their friends and family could gather when they came to visit. Jen and Rob had come just a week or two ago, with little Jacob and their adorable baby daughter Stephanie, who would be celebrating her first birthday soon. And Stumpy had been there too, of course. Bruce had been so happy to meet his old friend again and had shared the secret of where the best place to be was— under the big wooden table—especially when there were children on the benches who always dropped lots of food.

'We need a photo of Nico and Frankie,' Rosa declared. 'With Paolo. For Mamma.' She shook her head and sighed loudly. 'You'd think Paolo was her favourite grandchild, but we all know that I'm the family favourite so that makes my children the favourites too, doesn't it?'

Frankie caught Nico's gaze and shared a grin. Not that either of them would dare contradict Rosa, but they both knew that their baby was clearly the favourite. He was perfect, wasn't he?

She went to gently remove her son from her *nonna*'s arms and her grandmother gave her a knowing look as she relinquished the baby.

'I was right, wasn't I, Francesca?' she said. 'You just needed to find a nice Italian boy and settle down and have your own *bambino*. What took you so long?'

'I had to find the perfect man, Nonna.' Frankie smiled. 'I couldn't settle for anything less.'

And then she turned, with their precious baby in her arms, and walked towards Nico. The voices and laughter of their extended family were behind her as Giovanni prepared to take a photo of the new parents but all Frankie could see was the look in Nico's eyes.

The love that was becoming more and more like a physical touch as every step took her closer to this man she loved so much.

She would treasure the photo that was about to be taken. One day, when she was a *nonna* herself, she would be able to find it amongst so many other memories of the life she'd dreamed of having. She'd show it to Nico and they would smile at each other.

'What a wonderful day that was…'

'*Sì*. It was *perfetto*…'

* * * * *

*If you missed the previous story in the
Paramedics and Pups duet, then check out*

Her Off-Limits Single Dad
by Marion Lennox

*And if you enjoyed this story, check
out these other great reads from
Alison Roberts*

Fling with the Doc Next Door
Secret Son to Change His Life
How to Rescue the Heart Doctor

All available now!